GRILLED RYE MURDER

THE DARLING DELI SERIES, BOOK 16

PATTI BENNING

SUMMER PRESCOTT BOOKS PUBLISHING

CHAPTER ONE

The humid summer air swirled through the propped-open doors of the deli, bringing in the sweet scents of freshly cut grass and fried dough from the new donut shop down the street. Moira Darling put down her paint roller and took a step back, enjoying the breeze while casting a critical eye on her work. Darling's DELIcious Delights was getting a paint job, and to save money, the deli owner had decided to do it herself. Not even halfway through with the project, and she was already regretting her decision. It was a *hot* summer, and the strange thumping sound affecting the deli's air conditioning left the inside of the building too warm and swampy with paint fumes.

The repairman is coming tomorrow, she reminded herself. *By the time we reopen, the air will be back on. All I have to do is finish painting this evening, and the deli will be like new when the customers come back.*

She was just reaching for the roller again when a familiar convertible pulled into the parking lot. It was her twenty-one-year-old daughter, Candice. *Almost twenty-two,* she thought. *Where does the time go?* Moira watched as the young woman got out of her car, tucking a few strands of her straight, golden-blonde hair behind her ears before reaching into the back seat for a large box fan.

"Thanks for bringing that," Moira said, dropping the roller back into the paint as her daughter came inside. "I've been melting in here."

"Ugh, I don't see how you can stand it. It's like a furnace." The young woman placed the fan in a corner and plugged it in. "At least this will blow some of the paint fumes out. I don't know if it will help with the heat too much."

"It already feels better," Moira said, standing in front of the fan. "You're a lifesaver, sweetie."

"Do you want me to stay and help? Logan's watching the candy shop, so I've got a few hours if you need me."

"That would be amazing. Jenny and Cameron are going to come by at five after they're done catering Mrs. Brodeshire's baby shower, and they'll help me finish up, but things will go much more quickly with another person painting right now. Hang on, I've got an extra roller in the kitchen."

She brought her daughter out a fresh paint roller and smiled as she watched the young woman pull the beautiful diamond engagement ring off her finger and slip it into a pocket.

"I don't want to get paint on it," Candice told her mother.

"I don't blame you. It's gorgeous. Eli has good taste... in rings, and in women."

Her daughter grinned. Eli had proposed to her a month ago, and Moira hadn't seen a single frown on the young woman's face since. *We might not be a normal family, but we're definitely a happy one,* the deli owner thought as she picked up her own roller and began to start painting again.

Jenny and Cameron were Moira's two newest employees. She had hired them late last fall, when the deli had been slammed with holiday catering requests. They rarely worked at the counter; instead, it was their job to handle the catering events from start to finish. Jenny, a quiet brunette, had just moved to town when Moira hired her, and had quickly settled in. Cameron, a cheerful and outgoing redhead, had applied for the job soon after the young woman had begun her work; Moira was convinced that he was in love with the girl, although if Jenny knew it, she didn't let it show. Between the two of them, they had lightened the deli owner's work load considerably, and she would have done just about anything to keep them working there.

The work went much more quickly with Candice helping. The new paint, a light green color, looked amazing, and Moira wondered why she hadn't done this before. *Things have been going so well since David and I got engaged*, she thought. The memory of his proposal brought a smile to her lips. She was still just as certain of her answer as she had been when he had asked her almost a year ago. *Yes.* Yes, she wanted to spend the rest of her life with him. Yes, she wanted to wake up every morning with him beside her. Yes, she wanted to marry him.

Saying yes had been the easy part. Planning the wedding was fun, but it was also full of tough decisions to make. Her first wedding had been traditional, held inside a church with her close friends and family. This wedding—her second and *last* wedding—she wanted to be special. Her parents had passed away years ago, so she had to rely on her friends and daughter for help. David was the one she really counted on, though. He had been at her side for everything; finding a venue, considering flowers, choosing food and wine for the wedding dinner... he had even been the one to book kennel reservations for Maverick and Keeva while they went on their honeymoon.

I can't believe I'm getting married, she thought for the thousandth time since he had slid the ring on her finger. After the honeymoon, he was going to move into her house with her, and she had already begun clearing out the second bedroom for him to use as office space. They had discussed buying a bigger house together, but a cursory search online hadn't shown any promising homes for sale in the area. Moira was secretly glad; she was in love with her little stone house in the woods, and didn't want to move unless she happened to find another house that she loved just as much.

By the time Jenny and Cameron returned with the refrigerated food truck, Moira and Candice were painting the last wall. The deli owner was amazed at the difference the new paint had made, and couldn't wait for her customers to see it when the restaurant reopened at noon tomorrow. They had only been closed for three days for renovations, but it seemed like ages to her. The deli was more than just a hobby; it was her pride and joy and her main source of income. July was right in the middle of their busiest season, when tourists came from all over to enjoy the beautiful beaches of Lake Michigan, only twenty minutes away from the small town of Maple Creek. Closing up for renovations now had been a hard choice, but she really wanted everything to be done by the time of her wedding, so she wouldn't have to worry about it while she was on her honeymoon.

It took them another two hours to finish touching up the paint and replace the bistro tables and chairs along the walls. Moira tore down the sheets of protective plastic from over the register and glass counters, while Candice and Jenny peeled the painter's tape away from the moulding. Cameron washed the paint rollers and tray in the big stainless steel sink, carefully squeezing them out before setting them out to dry.

At long last, they were done. The walls were painted, the deli was clean, and the only thing left to do was to get the air conditioning fixed before her customers returned. All in all, it had been a very successful few days, though she couldn't deny that she was eager to get back to her normal routine.

"Do you want to join Eli and me for dinner tomorrow night?" Candice asked on her way out. "We're going to eat with Reggie. He still isn't doing so well, but his nurse says that he always seems a lot more energetic after we're there."

"Oh, I wish I could," Moira said. "But I promised David I'd have dinner with him at the Grill to cele-brate the completion of the new renovations. I've been so busy with all of this—" she gestured at the newly painted deli "—that we've barely seen each other all week. Maybe I could make next Sunday's dinner, instead?"

"Okay, I'll tell him that you wanted to come, but already had plans," her daughter said. "I know he loves seeing you. He thinks you and David are the coolest people ever."

The deli owner chuckled at that as she locked up behind them. Reginald, called Reggie by his friends, was the grandfather of Eli, Candice's fiancé. He lived at the local assisted-living home, and had helped Moira get to the bottom of two mysterious murders. From what she gathered, he was constantly on the lookout for more crimes to investigate; she was secretly glad that he hadn't found any. She was enjoying her quiet lifestyle, and didn't want to see it end any time soon.

"Any interesting plans for the rest of the week?" her daughter asked, leaning against the convertible that had been her birthday present from Moira and David the year before.

"Oh, not really," the deli owner said. "Which is a good thing. We've got mostly everything figured out for the wedding, so I'll hopefully be able to take a few days to relax before the next crisis. I do have a meeting with Zander the day after tomorrow—the deli's liquor license just got approved, and I've got to tell him the good news."

Zander was one of the farmers that she did business with. He also owned a microbrewery, and wanted her to start selling some of his beers and ales at the deli. She hadn't been completely on board with it at first, but he had been a good business partner and she figured that it wouldn't hurt to do this small favor for him. Besides, David was a fan of Zander's Pine Mountain Ale; she was certain he would appreciate being able to grab a bottle whenever he stopped by the deli.

"It's awesome that the deli's branching out even more," Candice said with a smile. "This place has changed so much over the last couple of years. It's amazing what you've done."

Moira agreed. Even though she had been there for every twist and turn the deli had taken as it grew, she was still shocked sometimes at how different the little shop was from how it had been when she first opened it. *These have been an amazing few years,* she thought. *But now I'm ready to start a new chapter to my life. I only hope that what lies ahead of me will be just as amazing as everything I've already been through.*

CHAPTER TWO

"Whoa, you two. Slow down. You almost trampled the arugula."

Moira gathered her trowel and bucket, which was now filled with weeds, and stood up. Maverick and Keeva, who had just run helter-skelter through her garden, stared at her guiltily from a few feet away.

"Oh, come here. I forgive you." She gave each dog a quick scratch behind the ears before heading towards her porch. "It's better than the time you ate *all* of the sugar snap peas off the vine. Who would have thought that two big carnivores like you two would have such a taste for veggies?"

Maverick, a black-and-tan German shepherd, cocked his head, his long tongue flopping out the side of his mouth. Keeva, a huge gray Irish wolfhound, was more dignified. She blinked her big brown eyes, then shoved her muzzle into her owner's hand for more skritches. Moira chuckled. It was hard to stay mad at either of them, even after they did something wrong. She loved them fiercely, and had never once regretted adopting the two of them. They were her constant companions around the house, and she felt safer knowing they were there.

It's a good thing David likes dogs, she thought as she brought her gardening tools inside and began washing up. *They'll love having him around all of the time once we're married.*

Thoughts of her fiancé made her glance at the clock; she only had half an hour left before he would be there to pick her up. If she wanted to wear something other than her gardening jeans and old tee shirt on their date, then she had better hurry up.

She had just put the finishing touches on her makeup when a knock at the door sounded. She could hear the dogs whining happily downstairs, and smiled. David and Candice were the only two people they didn't bark at; somehow they must recognize the way each car sounded when it pulled up.

"Come on in," she shouted. "I'm almost ready."

A minute later she walked down the stairs to find the man she loved sitting on her couch with both dogs half on his lap.

"I think they missed me," he said with a grin.

"Of course they did. You're their favorite person in the world... but look, they're getting you all furry."

She gave him a quick kiss, then handed him the lint roller—an essential tool in her house. The dogs, back on the floor, watched with interest as she walked to the kitchen. She returned with two treats, which she handed to each of them in turn.

"Be good, you two," she said. "I'll be back in a couple of hours."

The dogs ignored her words, instead sniffing at her hands for more treats. When they didn't find anything, Keeva heaved a big sigh and lay down on the rug in the living room, while Maverick stood by the front door hopefully, as he always did when Moira went somewhere.

"I think he wants to come," said David with a laugh.

"Denise may be one of my best friends, but I don't think even she would be too happy if I brought a dog in for dinner." She patted the German shepherd's head. "We'll go to the park sometime this week, all right, buddy?"

They left, closing and locking the door behind them. The deli owner glanced back when she was halfway to David's car, to see two furry faces staring longingly out of the living room window at her. She felt a swell of emotion for the dogs and for the man beside her. How could she be so lucky?

The Redwood Grill had made it through its first snowy Michigan winter by cutting back its hours and the number of employees, but now, in the middle of tourist season, business was back in full swing. Couples walked through the oak front doors arm in arm, and the hostess greeted each of them with a smile. The delicious scent of sizzling steak permeated the warm summer air around the restaurant, and Moira felt her stomach growl at the thought of the scrumptious food that awaited them inside. The Grill was her and David's traditional date

PATTI BENNING

spot—they had gone here nearly every week for a year and a half. The menu was changed up every month or two, which kept their dinners interesting, and everyone that worked there knew them by name.

"Your regular table's available, Ms. Darling, Mr. Morris," the hostess said. "Right this way."

She led them through the busy restaurant to a private booth in the back. David took the menus from her and Moira opened hers eagerly when he handed it over.

"Mmm, Denise updated the menus already," she said, looking at all of the new dishes being offered. "I don't know what to choose."

"I know what I'm getting," he said, giving her a sheepish grin. "The sirloin steak with a fried egg and mashed potatoes."

She laughed, shaking her head at what was one of many small differences between them. She loved trying all sorts of new food, even if it wasn't the sort of dish that she usually liked, but David tended to stick with his favorites. He loved steak, and didn't see any reason to risk trying something else that he might not like as much.

"Well, I think I'm going to go with the pesto and shrimp pasta," she said. "I've always loved the pesto here."

Within minutes, their waiter had brought them their drinks—white wine for Moira, and a pale ale for David—and had taken their order, as well as telling Moira that Denise would stop by in a little bit to say hello.

"It still amazes me that you two are friends," the private investigator said after tasting his ale.

"Why?" She was surprised. She and Denise had been friends for over a year, and had a lot in common. Both of them were in the food business, both had lost close family members, and both of them had been in bad relationships. Denise had recently finalized her divorce with her husband, who had cheated on her multiple times with different women, and Moira was the only one out of their group of friends that really understood what she had been going through.

"Well, because she's so competitive," David said. "Your deli has been doing such good business, it must be impacting her sales quite a bit."

"I don't know... the deli isn't really a restaurant, not like the Grill is. We have a couple of specials available each day, and some warm food in the morning, but other than that we mostly just sell cold cuts and cheeses." She took a sip of her wine, wondering secretly if David had a point. Her business *had* been growing lately. Was she stealing customers away from Denise? She didn't really want to think about it just then; she wanted to enjoy this date with her fiancé. Casting around for a change in subject, her eyes landed on the ale that he was drinking, and she brightened.

"Oh, did I tell you that I'm meeting with Zander tomorrow to discuss selling some of the beer and ale from his microbrewery?"

"Really?" David grinned. "I've got to admit; I've been pretty excited ever since you told me you got your liquor license. Zander's really gifted, and it will be great for him to have some local exposure."

"It feels good to help another small business," she agreed. "He's been a good friend this past year, and I've never had one complaint about the produce that he delivers. I'm sure his brewery products will be just as high quality."

"You know," David mused, "you could think of expanding. The deli's doing so well, and Darrin's a great manager. You could open up a second shop in another town and—"

"Wait," Moira cut in. "Are you talking about... moving?"

"It's just something to think about," he said with a shrug. "I'm open to it if you are."

She frowned, turning the idea over in her head. It wasn't a *terrible* idea, in fact from a business standpoint it was a pretty good one. It was the thought of leaving all of her friends here in Maple Creek that made her so hesitant. She had gotten so close to Martha, Denise, and Karissa. And how could she even think of moving farther away from Candice? Sure, her daughter had her own business and her own house now, but... she still needed her mother. And Moira needed her daughter.

On the other hand, the prospect of opening a whole new deli in a new town was a tempting one. She wouldn't make as many mistakes this time around as she had when she first opened Darling's DELIcious Delights, and she would already have a strong reputation to stand on. Darrin *was* a great manager....

"Let's talk more about this later," she said with a smile as their food came. "Right now, I want to focus on the wedding and our future together. Have you thought any more about where you want to go for our honeymoon?"

"As long as you're there," he said, taking her hand, "I could go anywhere."

CHAPTER THREE

She set out for her meeting with Zander the next morning with a yawn and a thermos full of coffee. She and David had stayed up late talking about their plans for the future, and she was exhausted. *Next time I have an eight AM meeting, I need to go to bed earlier,* she thought. Still, despite her fatigue, she had had a lot of fun the evening before. There was something wonderful about being able to completely let go and be yourself with another person.

Zander's farm was only about half an hour away, and the drive was a nice one: rolling fields dotted with old barns and the occasional pasture with horses, cows, and in one case, alpacas. Keeping up a good relationship with her suppliers was important to her; not only did they tend to give her better prices when they knew her personally, but it also made it easier to ask for the occasional rush delivery or delayed payment. It was worth the occasional trip out to the countryside, especially to see Zander. He was younger than most of the other farmers that she worked with, and got along well with everyone at the deli. Not only that, but his dog, a little yellow lab mix, was one of the puppies that Moira had raised last year. She was always happy to see the little pup, who had a permanently cheerful disposition and a tail that never stopped wagging.

When she pulled up to Zander's old farmhouse, she took one last swig of coffee from her thermos, shut her engine off, then started across the lawn to the large, square, windowless building that the farmer used as both his office and his brewery. She paused for a moment when she saw a large black van that she didn't recognize parked near his house. Did he have company? *He didn't call to cancel our meeting,* she told herself. *And he's nearly as much of a workaholic as I am. Even if he has someone over, he'll probably be in the brewery by now.*

She wasn't surprised when he didn't answer her knock on the door; he had a tendency to listen to loud music while in the back working on his brews. After rapping on the door once more, hard enough to make her knuckles sting, she gave up and let herself in. No doubt he would remember the time and come up front to his office soon enough.

"Hey, Flower," she said as she opened the door. The little yellow dog rushed up to her, her entire body wriggling with joy. Sunflower, called Flower for short, had been the runt of the litter and had never gotten quite as big as her litter-mates, but didn't let her small size stop her. Moira knew that the dog went everywhere with Zander, who owned two farms and a small herd of dairy cattle.

"Where's your owner, hmm?" she asked, crouching down to pet the dog. She was rarely anywhere but at Zander's side.

27

The dog whined and turned her head to lick at Moira's hand. The deli owner frowned. Was that blood on the dog's muzzle?

"Did you cut yourself on something, sweetie?" she murmured. She gently turned the dog's head to the side, her eyes searching the dog's face for any sign of an injury. She didn't see one, but perhaps the dog had somehow managed to bite her tongue or lip.

"Let's go find Zander," she said.

To her surprise, the dog gave another low whine, then dashed off—not towards the heavy door that lead back to the brewery, but to the left, where Zander's office was. Moira followed the dog to the office door, which was open just enough for the dog to slip inside. The deli owner pushed it open the rest of the way, then paused at the threshold to the dark room. She slapped blindly at the wall for a few seconds before she found the light switch and flicked it on. What she saw made her gasp in horror and stumble backwards.

She leaned against the wall outside of the office, her eyes screwed shut as she told herself that she must have seen wrong. Gathering her courage, she poked her head around the corner and saw that she hadn't been wrong at all.

Zander was sitting in the chair at his desk, his head tilted unnaturally to the side, and his arms hanging limply off of the arms of the chair. He had been shot twice; once in the shoulder, and once in the center of his chest. Blood from the wound in his shoulder was still slowly dripping down his right arm to pool on the floor beneath his outstretched fingers.

Flower licked her owner's hand once, then looked back at Moira as if asking for help. *That must be where the blood on her muzzle came from*, the deli owner thought, her brain still reeling from the shock. Zander, dead? Or... could he possibly still be alive? She didn't see how he could be, but she had heard of people surviving unbelievable things before; a fall from an airplane, or an iron rod through the skull.

Feeling numb, she walked slowly towards the man in the chair. She touched his neck with shaking fingers, feeling for a pulse, but feeling nothing. *His body isn't cold yet*, the deli owner thought. *He can't have been dead for long.* She jerked her fingers, back, realizing that she was touching a corpse, then looked sadly at the man who had been her friend. Had he killed himself? It seemed impossible, but the thought of him being murdered seemed equally impossible. *If he killed himself, there would have to be a gun here*, she thought, her eyes raking his empty hands and lap. Where was it?

As if in answer to her question, a metallic clunk sounded from behind her. She spun around to see Flower trying to pick up a large black handgun from the floor. The muzzle of the gun slipped out of her mouth again and it fell to the floor with another thunk. Moira rushed over and gingerly grabbed the gun before the dog managed to pull the trigger. Holding it carefully out in front of her by her fingertips she set it on the table near Zander. Flower trotted over and began licking Zander's hand again, whining all the while.

"Stop that," Moira said. "Come over here, Flower. Let him be."

The sight of the little dog licking the dead man's hand seemed gruesome to her. Didn't the dog understand that he was gone? It wasn't right for her to keep bothering him like that. It wasn't until she felt something wet on her cheeks that she realized she was crying.

I have to call the police, she thought, wiping her eyes with the back of her hand. *There's no one else here to do it.* Calling Flower over to her again, she walked on unsteady legs back to the office doorway, where she had dropped her purse. It took her a moment to find her phone inside, and another couple of seconds to pull up the number for the local police station.

What am I doing? she thought, hanging up the phone after the first ring. *This is an emergency. I should be calling nine-one-one.* She punched in the three digits quickly, but hesitated. Off in the distance, she heard the faint wail of sirens, and they were drawing ever nearer.

Her skin prickled as the noise of the sirens reached a crescendo, then cut off. She heard the pop and crunch of tires on gravel, and rushed over to the exit to look outside. And ambulance and three police cars, lights flashing, were pulling to a stop in front of the brewery. *Someone must have heard the gunshots and called already*, she thought, taking a firm hold on Flower's collar as she slipped her phone into her pants' pocket.

A team of paramedics rushed towards the building. "He's in there," Moira called out, pointing towards the office with the hand that wasn't holding on to Flower. The men hurried past her without a word. Moira edged out of the building, hoping to get somewhere out of the way so she could call David, but a woman wearing khakis, a black button-down shirt, and a no-nonsense expression was approaching her from where the police cars were parked. It was Detective Wilson, one of the two senior detectives at the Maple Creek Police Department. The other, Detective Jefferson, was nowhere to be seen. *This isn't good*, she thought. Jefferson knew her well enough to know that she was just in the wrong place at the wrong time, but Detective Wilson had never liked her, and she could already see the suspicion on the other woman's face.

"Ms. Darling, I'm going to need you to come with me," the detective said. She glanced down at Flower. "Is this your dog?"

"No," Moira said. "She's... she was Zander's. But I raised her, and I'd be happy to take care of her for now."

Wilson shook her head, then gestured one of the officers over. Moira recognized him as Officer Catto, who she had spoken to a few times over the last year. He seemed to like her, and she felt a bit better knowing that there was at least one person there who wouldn't automatically assume the worst of her.

"Catto, crank the AC in the cruiser and put the dog in the back, then see if you can find a leash for it somewhere. We'll take it back to the station, check it over for evidence, then see if we can't contact the victim's next of kin."

"Her name's Flower," Moira called out as Catto walked away with the dog. She bit her lip, hoping that Flower would be comfortable and happy during her stay with the police, then turned her attention back to Detective Wilson.

"I'm happy to answer any questions—"

"Ms. Darling, you are under arrest for the murder of Zander Marsh. You have the right to remain silent..."

The deli owner went limp with disbelief as the detective turned her around, pulled her wrists together, and tightened a cold pair of handcuffs around them.

CHAPTER FOUR

Moira sat on the corner of the thin mattress in the holding cell, staring blankly at one of the white walls. Everything in the cell was white, from the plastic-lined sheets on the mattress, to the painted iron bars, to the tile floor. Only the small sink and toilet in the opposite corner stood out; they were a gleaming, cold stainless steel.

What am I doing here? she thought for the thousandth time that night. She had sat in stunned silence in the back of the police cruiser that drove her from Zander's farm, certain that at any moment the officer would realize that her arrest had been nothing but a horrible mistake. Certainly she hadn't expected to be processed and locked in a holding cell in Maple Creek's tiny police station.

At least they let me call David and Candice. Her only experience with jail up to this point had been what she'd seen on television crime shows. She had been surprised that she was allowed to make several calls, and even more surprised when an officer whom she didn't recognize had brought her a bag of fast food a few hours later.

She had been treated well enough, but that didn't change the frustrating fact that no one had actually told her anything useful about when she might be able to get out. She hadn't heard back from David, who had promised to get in touch with Detective Jefferson and explain the situation to him, and when Detective Wilson stopped by a few hours before, she had done nothing but ask Moira a few basic questions, like what she had done earlier that morning and if she had an alibi.

"I can't believe I'm going to spend the night in a jail cell," she muttered, staring up at the small window set high into the wall of the cell. Her cell phone had been taken from her when she was processed, so she had no way to tell the time, but it was dark out. *I must have been here for at least twelve hours already.* Spending another twelve there was a sobering thought, but until she heard back from David, there was nothing she could do.

The deli owner lay down on the bumpy mattress and pulled the scratchy blanket over herself. The lights in the cell were off, but the hall lights were on, and they were bright enough that it would be hard to sleep. Wide-awake and worried, Moira lay there for hours until she finally sank into a dreamless slumber.

A loud clang awoke her a few hours later. The sun had risen, but her sleep had been poor, and she felt groggy. It took her a moment to remember where she was, then it all came back to her at once. Zander was dead... and Detective Wilson thought that she had killed him.

Another clang made her jump, and she sat bolt upright in bed. The sound of people talking could be heard beyond the doors to the holding cell area. Someone was coming.

Feeling a sudden surge of hope, Moira leapt off the bed. Was that David's voice?

Sure enough, moments later the private investigator walked in. He was followed closely by Detective Jefferson, Moira's friend and the senior detective at the Maple Creek police station.

"Oh my goodness," she said, rushing up to the bars. "I'm so glad to see you two."

David came forward and took her hand as Detective Jefferson approached to unlock the cell door.

"How are you holding up?" her fiancé asked her, his gaze searching her face. She knew he wasn't asking just about her overnight stay in the holding cell, but about Zander's death as well. He knew the two of them had been friends.

"I still can't believe it... none of this feels real to me," she said. She glanced over at the police detective. "What's going on? Am I being released?"

"That's... complicated," David told her. "We'll go over it somewhere more comfortable, though." His face full of concern, he gave her hand a reassuring squeeze before releasing her hand and stepping back as Jefferson swung her cell door open.

"Come on," the detective said. "Fresh coffee and muffins are waiting in my office."

It felt good to be back in more familiar territory. Moira had been in Detective Jefferson's office more times than she could count, and the familiar large wooden desk and comfortable leather chairs were definite improvements over the spartan holding cell that she had spent the last day in. She sipped her coffee gratefully and listened as the two men took turns telling her what had happened after her arrest.

"As soon as I got off the phone with you, I got in touch with Detective Jefferson," David explained. "He was out of town at the time, but the second I told him what had happened, he rushed back."

Moira shot a grateful glance at the detective, who smiled at her. "When I heard that you had been arrested for murder, something just didn't sit right. You've been brought in for questioning plenty of times before, but you've never been guilty of anything, not even a speeding ticket. As far as I'm concerned, you're an upstanding citizen, and someone who has really helped this town out multiple times." The detective sighed. "Wilson's a good detective, but she's never approved of our... unorthodox relationship. This is a hard situation for me, you have to understand. She's the only other detective here, and I can't just go against her completely, but I also can't let someone I know to be innocent stay locked up. Luckily, I've done a couple of favors for the district judge, so he was willing to do me one in return. We got your charges reduced—"

"Wait, I'm being charged with something?" Moira cut in, stunned. She put down her coffee, her stomach suddenly feeling turbulent.

"Yes. Unfortunately, I can't get the charges completely cleared until we work through the case. But I did manage to get them reduced from second-degree murder to manslaughter—"

"Murder?" she squeaked, interrupting him for a second time. "But I didn't do it. I thought this was all some big mistake."

"We're still trying to figure out what's going on,"

43

David said. He turned in his seat to face her and took both of her hands. "Listen, I know you're innocent, and so does Detective Jefferson. But someone out there is doing their best to get you put away for Zander's murder. Didn't you wonder how the police showed up before you even got a chance to make a call?"

She nodded. "I thought one of the neighbors must have heard the gunshots and called it in."

The private investigator shook his head. "That's a reasonable assumption, but no. Moira, someone called the police and gave an eyewitness description of someone dressed exactly like *you* entering the brewery moments before he heard shots go off."

"W-what?"

"It's true," Jefferson said grimly. "That's why Detective Wilson arrested you on the spot."

Moira sat back in her chair, feeling faint. Had someone dressed exactly like her killed Zander? Or... was someone trying to frame her specifically? But how would they know what she was wearing?

"Did you see or hear anything strange when you got there?" David asked. "Or did you notice anyone following you earlier that morning?"

"No, I don't think so. I woke up, took care of the dogs, grabbed some coffee, then left for Zander's. I remember the roads out in the country being empty; if someone was following me, they would have had to be pretty far behind."

"How about when you got to his property?" he prodded. "From the description the witness gave, they must have had eyes on you at some point that morning."

"I didn't see anyone else there," she said. "Except that big black van parked behind his house that I didn't remember seeing before."

The private investigator turned to Detective Jefferson with raised eyebrows. The detective flipped through a sheaf of notes, then shook his head.

"We don't have anything on file about a van being there," he told her. "The only other vehicle was a blue pickup truck that was registered to Zander. Can you describe the vehicle in any more detail? Did you happen to see the license plate?"

"I don't remember," she said, frustrated. "It was just a big black cargo van with tinted windows. I didn't think too much of it at the time; I just thought he might have had guests or something."

"Don't worry, that's understandable. I'll add a note

about it to the case file, all right? We'll do what we can to figure out who it belongs to."

She nodded, feeling tense and emotional. "So I'm really a murder suspect? What happens now?"

"Well, like I said, I managed to get the charges dropped from murder to manslaughter," the detective told her.

"I don't understand the difference. They're still saying I killed someone, aren't they?"

"Murder is premeditated," he explained. "Manslaughter is done in the heat of the moment. Bail for a murder suspect requires a court hearing, but the judge can set bail for a manslaughter suspect without one. It was the only thing I could think of to get you out of here as quickly as possible without you having to go to court for an arraignment. The fact that the gun found at the crime scene was registered to Zander himself made it easier; you obviously didn't bring the weapon from home planning to kill him."

"Does this mean that I'm free to go once I pay bail?" Moira asked. "What happens then?"

"Well, you won't be able to leave the state, and you'll have to show up for your court date—if this goes to court. I hope to figure out who the real killer is before then, of course. Other than that, you'll be able to live your life as you normally do."

It could be worse, she thought. *David and Detective Jefferson are the best investigators I know. With both of them trying to find the real killer, I'm sure my name will be cleared in no time.*

"So how much is my bail?"

48

"Sixty thousand dollars," Jefferson said.

Moira spluttered.

"There's no way I can pay that!"

"I know. I was going to start looking for a bail bond agency, but about an hour ago, I got an interesting call," David said. He exchanged a look with the detective.

"What?" she asked, looking between them.

"Someone already paid your bail," her fiancé told her. "All sixty thousand dollars of it. And whoever it was, didn't leave a name."

CHAPTER FIVE

"I just don't understand... who could have done it?"

It was hours later. Their talk with Detective Jefferson done, Moira had gotten her personal items back from a grouchy woman at the front desk, and David was driving her home through a sudden summer downpour.

"I'm just as much at a loss as you are," he said.

"That's a lot of money."

"I know." To her surprise, his voice was grim. "There's definitely something going on here that we don't understand."

"What do we do now? How do we even start figuring out who really killed Zander?"

"We don't," he said sternly, shooting her a glance. "Let Detective Jefferson and I handle this, all right? I know it's going to be hard for you to sit back and keep out of the investigation, but that's exactly what you have to do. I don't want you giving anyone anything to use against you. If you're caught snooping around his property, it could be bad."

"I won't do anything like that," she told him. "But maybe I can talk with some of the other people that worked with him. They might have noticed if he was acting strange. One of the ladies I buy specialty bread from gets her wheat and rye from him. That might be a good place to start."

"Okay," he said with a sigh. "If it will keep you out of trouble, go ahead. Just remember—don't draw attention to yourself. One fingerprint in the wrong place, and the prosecutors could have a real case against you."

"Oh! Um..."

"What?" he glanced over at her again. "What did you do?"

"I *might* have touched the gun that was used to kill Zander," she said. "As in, I picked it up and put it on the desk."

"*What?*" The car swerved.

"Flower kept trying to pick it up!" she exclaimed. "I didn't want it to go off or something. I wasn't thinking straight. I had just found my friend brutally murdered, for goodness sake. I didn't even remember that I did it until just now."

She looked over at David, who was gripping the steering wheel with white knuckles. She knew what he was thinking; first, someone had called the police to report a murder, and had described her to a T as the suspect. Now the police were going to find her fingerprints on the gun used in the crime. *At this rate, it won't be long before I'm back in that cell.*

"You need to call Jefferson," he said at last. "Right away. Tell him anything else you can think of while you're at it. I'm going to do my best to get us home through this monsoon without crashing."

The ensuing phone call with the detective wasn't the most pleasant one that she had ever had, but by the time it was over, she was glad that she had remembered about touching the gun before they ran the thing for prints. At least she would look less guilty this way.

"This is terrible," she groaned as David pulled into her driveway. "The wedding is only a couple of weeks away. I can't deal with all of this on top of that. Any how are we supposed to go away for our honeymoon if I can't leave the state?"

"I'm sure it will all be figured out by then," he said. "And if not, we'll have a perfectly nice honeymoon somewhere in Michigan."

"Just as long as we don't have to hold the wedding in a prison." She bit her lip. "I'm really afraid, David. What if the police don't find the real killer? What if whoever made the fake call planted more evidence against me?"

"Easy now. Detective Jefferson—and even Detective Wilson, even though she doesn't like you—they're both good detectives. You're innocent; no amount of fake evidence or fake witnesses will change that.

There's no such thing as a perfect crime; the real killer will have left some evidence behind, and one of us *will* find it. Now, let's go in and see how your daughter fared with the dogs last night." He kissed her on the cheek and gave her an encouraging smile. "I love you. Everything will be fine."

Maverick and Keeva greeted Moira at the door, nearly trampling her in their excitement. She felt a swell of happiness wash over her as she let each dog give her kisses. They didn't know or care that she was a suspected murderer—they were simply happy that she was home. Her daughter, on the other hand, was a different story.

"Oh my goodness, Mom! I can't believe they actually arrested you. You wouldn't hurt anyone."

The second the dogs switched their attention from Moira to David, Candice flung herself at her mother and wrapped her arms around her.

"It's okay, sweetie. I'm out now." The deli owner gave her daughter a squeeze in return. "Thanks so much for coming here and taking care of these two crazies." She glanced affectionately back at the dogs. "It was a relief not to have to worry about them."

"It was the least I could do, Mom. I just can't believe that you went through all of that. How did you manage to get out? How did you afford the bail?"

Moira glanced at David. She had no idea how much Candice knew or didn't know. Everything had happened so quickly while she was in jail that she still felt out of the loop.

"I told Candice how much your bail was to see if she could help me come up with a solution," he explained. "She's a successful businesswoman just like her mom, after all. I thought she might have some good ideas."

"I didn't though," the young woman admitted. "The only thing I could think of was the same thing David had already thought of—try to find a bond agency."

"Well, thankfully it wasn't needed. Apparently, someone anonymous paid the bail on my behalf."

"Wow," Candice said, her eyes going wide. "That's a lot of money. You don't have any clue who did it?"

"Nope. Who all knew about it?"

"Well, everyone at the deli," her daughter said. "I was hanging out with Allison when David called, and I didn't think to ask her not to tell the others."

"Plus me, and probably a few people at the police station," David added. "It's not exactly a small pool of people to choose from."

"I don't see how anyone working at the police station or the deli could *afford* that sort of payment," Moira said. "Wait... David, did you...?"

The private investigator grinned. "I wish I could take the credit for it, but no. Unfortunately, I don't have any secret riches hidden away somewhere. What you see is what you get."

"That's more than enough for me," the deli owner said with a smile. He kissed her, a quick brush of his lips against hers.

"Eww," Candice said, wrinkling her nose. "At least wait until I'm gone to do that. You're awesome, David, but I still don't want to see you and my mom kiss."

"Sorry," he said with a chuckle. "I should get going, actually. I'm going to spend the rest of the day seeing what I can dig up on Zander Marsh. The guy was a

PATTI BENNING

rising star in the microbrewery world—maybe he stepped on some toes in his journey towards the top."

"Let me know if you find anything?"

"Of course."

She smiled, glad that he wasn't going to try to wall her out of the investigation as he had done in the past. "I'll follow you outside so I can kiss you goodbye without offending my dear daughter."

Candice rolled her eyes, and Moira laughed. The last two days had been a challenge, but she certainly had an amazing support system to help her through it.

CHAPTER SIX

At the deli the next morning, Moira was faced with an unpleasant surprise. A news van was waiting in the parking lot, and the cameraman and reporter were standing right outside the locked front doors. Somehow they must have found out about her arrest. The only question was; how much did they know?

"Ms. Darling?" the reporter said, rushing forward as she opened her car door. "My name is Brendan Anaheim. I'd love the chance to interview you about your recent arrest and subsequent release. I work for Beyond News, an up-and-coming local station. We bring in stories from Traverse City all the way up to Mackinaw City. A story like this would turn Maple

Creek from a sleepy tourist town into the hot spot of the year."

"I'm sorry," Moira told him. "But I really need to get inside and start working." She looked over at the cameraman, not sure whether he was recording or not. The last thing she wanted was to be on the evening news.

"It will only take a moment, Ms. Darling. Just imagine the headlines! *Fifty-Year-Old Woman Brutally Kills Farmer: Who's Next?* We would get thousands of viewers. You'd become famous overnight."

"I'm not fifty," the deli owner snapped, losing patience with the man. "And I didn't kill him." She made to step around him, but he backpedaled, keeping himself between her and the deli door.

"So you're going to claim innocence? Even better! Let

the viewers hear your side of the story. Let the public hear the truth!"

He was the most exuberant man that she had ever met, and she was sure that whatever she told him would be twisted to match what he wanted his viewers to see... but still, what he said gave her pause. Maybe it *would* be a good idea to get her side of the story out there, especially if rumors that she had killed Zander were going around already.

"I'll think about it," she told him at last. "But right now, I really do need to get to work."

"Of course! Here's my card. Call me any time of the day or night to set up an interview. The sooner the better. How about tonight? Tomorrow morning? I could do lunch—"

"I don't know when yet," she told him, cutting him off. "I still need to wrap my brain around everything that's going on. Thank you for the card. I'll call you when I'm ready."

With that she stepped around him, quickly unlocked the deli's front door, and hurried inside. She was completely shaken by what had happened—how had news about her arrest gotten out already?—but thought that considering the situation, she had handled the news team's ambush well.

She got the breakfast cookies and mini quiches in the oven with time to spare, and spent the last few minutes before the deli officially opened getting the ingredients ready for the lunch selection: a creamy chicken and gnocchi soup and bean sprout salad sandwiches on rye. One thing she loved about owning her own restaurant was the freedom to play with new dishes whenever she wanted. She enjoyed making something new almost every single day, and her customers seemed to enjoy the variety as well. Of course, some of her soups did so well that people would ask for them specifically when they came in. She made extra of her most popular soups and sold it in small frozen containers.

That's what's so nice about being a small business, she thought as she pulled the tray of cranberry and white chocolate breakfast cookies out of the oven. *I can work with my customers individually, instead of being forced to stick to some corporate policy.*

She was just putting the finishing touches on a platter of quiches when she heard the bell on the deli's front door jingle, signaling the arrival of one of her employees. She assumed it was Meg, who was scheduled to work with her that morning, so was surprised when Jenny walked in.

"Oh dear, what's wrong?" Moira asked, the sight of the woman's red puffy eyes and tear-streaked face making her forget all about the quiches.

"I—I just heard about Zander," Jenny said. Her voice was tremulous, and Moira realized she must have been crying all night.

"Did you know him very well?" the deli owner asked, guiding the young woman over to a stool. She understood how shocking it could be when someone you knew died suddenly, but Jenny's reaction seemed over the top. As far as she knew, they had only met a few times when Zander dropped off last-minute deliveries for some of their catering jobs.

"Yeah, I dated him for a couple of months," Jenny said, sniffling. Moira, though surprised by this news, just patted the girl on the back. "We had just started really talking and spending time together again. I thought it was weird when he didn't answer my calls yesterday... but I never imagined he was dead."

"How did you find out?"

"There was a news story. I just caught the end of it." Her eyes filled with tears. "I didn't want to believe it, but the same story was online too."

"I'm so sorry, Jenny. That must have been horrible."

"They were saying that *you* killed him, Ms. D! I don't believe them, of course, but I had to come over here and ask... what really happened?"

Moira told her everything, not leaving out even the smallest detail in case the young woman, as Zander's friend, recognized something that she, David, and the police had overlooked. She was still surprised at the revelation that the two had dated, but the more she thought about it, the more sense that it made. Zander was only about five years older than Jenny, after all, and Jenny's family had a winery in the lower part of the state. They must have had a fair amount in common.

"What did they say about me?" the deli owner asked at last. "How do they even know that I was arrested? What station was this?"

"Um, I don't know. I was just flipping through channels. It might have been called Beyond News or something? Not one of the big ones."

Moira frowned. She wasn't surprised. That reporter must have had some sort of source inside the police station. *Now all I need is for them to find out about my bail being anonymously posted, and they'll definitely have something to report about.*

"Is there anything you need, Jenny?" she asked at last. "I can give you time off, if you want. I know this is really rough for you."

"No, I think it's best if I keep working. Thanks though, Ms. D. I just... I wanted to hear what really happened from you, you know? At least it sounds like it was quick. I hope he didn't suffer much."

"I don't think he did," Moira said, the unpleasant image of Zander's still body and the bullet wounds rising in her memory. "I don't think he would have suffered much at all."

"What's going to happen to Flower?" the young woman asked. "I know he loved her a lot."

"I don't know, but I'll call the police station later today and see if I can find out. Would you want to take her?"

"I want to, but I can't," Jenny said regretfully. "I'm allergic to dogs. Nothing too bad, but having one around the house all the time would make me miserable."

"Well, I'll see what I can do. Go on and get some rest, Jenny. You look exhausted. I promise to keep you in the loop."

The question of Flower nagged at her all day. She had kept up with all six of the puppies over the last year, but the little yellow runt had always been her favorite. Did Zander have anyone lined up to take care of the pup? If not, would the police let her take the dog home with her? The last thing she wanted was to see Flower end up in the pound.

CHAPTER SEVEN

Despite the fact that she was out of jail on sixty thousand dollars' bail posted by a rich and mysterious benefactor, and was suspected of murdering a colleague and friend, life went on. Moira had a wedding to plan.

She'd gotten a lot done over the past few months, but there was still one glaring detail that she hadn't tackled yet; she needed a wedding dress. She was just about out of excuses to keep putting it off. There was no way she was going to lose that ten pounds between now and the wedding, not with all of the stress eating that she had been doing. And being too busy was hardly an excuse when she herself worked up the deli's schedules. When her friends ganged up on her a couple of days after her arrest and told her that they were going wedding dress shopping with or without her, she finally gave in.

"I don't see why you put it off this long," Denise said. "If you find something that you want to modify a lot, you're not going to have time." She, Moira, Martha, and Karissa were all piled into the deli owner's green SUV, clutching iced coffees from their pit stop at the coffee shop, and surreptitiously brushing leftover breakfast cookie crumbs off their laps.

"I know. I should have done this ages ago." The deli owner groaned. "I was really hoping to lose that weight, though. I want to look good walking down the aisle."

"Moira, you look great," Martha said. "What are you talking about? Since when are you self-conscious?"

"I know it sounds stupid, but I'm terrified that when

David sees me walking towards him at the wedding, he's going to realize what a big mistake he's making and run out of the church. I wouldn't even blame him. I mean, look at me. I've got a muffin top, I've got wrinkles... and now I'm out on bail as a suspected murderer. What's he even thinking, marrying me?" She fell silent, embarrassed by her outburst, but glad that she had finally told her worries to someone.

"Moira, he loves you," Karissa said, reaching forward from the back seat to give the deli owner's shoulder a reassuring squeeze. "Trust me. You're the one for him."

"If he cared about those extra ten pounds you keep complaining about, then he wouldn't be worth marrying anyway," Martha pointed out. "And who *doesn't* have some wrinkles at our age? He knows that you didn't kill that guy. He's already stuck with you through a lot more."

"You guys are right," the deli owner said at last. "I

know deep down that David's not going anywhere... I guess this is just a case of pre-wedding jitters. Okay, I'm ready for this—let's go find that perfect wedding dress."

Both Maple Creek and Lake Marion had more than their fair share of consignment and antique shops. While Moira wasn't opposed to buying a new wedding dress, she wanted to look at some older ones first. Somehow the thought of buying a dress with history appealed to her; this wasn't her first wedding, after all. It shouldn't be the dress's either.

In her mind, she had envisioned herself walking into a consignment store, heading right to the back, and finding a gorgeous antique wedding dress to wear, that fit her perfectly and somehow made her look ten times more beautiful than she really was. The reality turned out to be a bit different.

"I forgot... just how... *tough*... these are to put on," Moira gasped as Martha gave a final tug on the back of the dress that she was lacing up. The deli owner waited as her friend tied the laces off.

"Not bad," the other woman said appraisingly.

"I don't know." The deli owner eyed herself in the mirror. The dress was so tight, it felt like she was wearing a corset. It was satin, with a scoop neckline and no train. Not too heavy, it would at least be feasible to wear at a summer wedding. "It's just... not quite right. I want something with more character."

"All right." Martha sighed and eyed the back of the dress. "Now to get it off again..."

It was hours before Moira finally spotted what she was looking for. The friends had exhausted the possibilities at the local consignment shops and had just entered the first antique shop on their list. It was a beautiful ivory dress with lace straps and a short train. Intricate designs were embroidered on the bodice, with real pearls on the neckline. The skirt flared out just the right amount without being overstated, and, best of all, it looked like it would fit her.

The woman running the shop let agreed to let her try it on in one of the back rooms. "We don't get many clothes in, so we don't have dressing rooms. That one's a real beauty, though, and we were happy to take it. Come on, right this way..."

The other three two woman wandered around the rest of the shop while Martha and Moira followed the shopkeeper into a dusty storage room. The deli owner ducked behind a stack of boxes to strip off her clothes in privacy, and stepped into the dress. Clasping it to her chest, she called her friend over to lace it up.

"Wow," Martha breathed, stepping back and taking a good look at the dress after she had finished. "I think you've found your dress."

Moira, eager to see, followed her friend out of the back room and looked at herself in a mirror set into the door of an old wardrobe. The antique shop owner bustled over to see, followed by Denise and Karissa.

"What do you think?" Martha asked her eagerly.

"It's... perfect," the deli owner breathed. The dress fit her like a second skin. She could breathe and move easily, but it had enough shape of its own to give her a waist. The neckline was modest, unlike some of the too-revealing dresses that she had tried on earlier in the day. She turned, admiring the back of the dress and the graceful train. This was a dress that she would be eager for David to see her in.

Martha undid the back of the dress and Moira hurried back into the storage room to change into her own clothes. She couldn't wait to show Candice the dress that she had found. It was everything she had hoped for, and more. *I'm glad I waited,* she thought as she pulled her own clam-digger jeans back on. *It was worth it to find something so beautiful to walk down the aisle in.*

She was putting the dress carefully back on its padded hanger when someone knocked on the storage room door.

"Moira? Your phone is ringing. It's that cop you're friends with."

Why is Detective Jefferson calling me now? she wondered, her heart beginning to pound as she hurried to get the dress settled on the hanger. *Did they get a break in the case?* She hurried out of the room and grabbed her phone from Martha, leaving the wedding dress with her friends so she could step outside and take the call.

"Hello?" she said when she answered it, bracing herself for bad news.

"Moira, I'm glad you answered. How are things going with you?"

"Good," she said. "I actually just found the perfect wedding dress."

"That's good. Has anyone been bothering you?"

"What do you mean?" she asked.

"Well, I saw a short clip on the news the other day, of you outside the deli talking to a reporter. They said you refused to comment at the time, but promised them an exclusive interview once you got your story straight. Those were their words, by the way. Not mine."

"Oh, that." She rubbed her hand across her face. "I

didn't promise them an interview, I just told them I'd think about it. And I didn't say anything about having to get my story straight first."

"I figured that was the case, but I wanted to check in. My professional opinion is that you stay far away from the media, Moira. Don't give them that interview, don't even say anything if they approach you again. They won't cast you in a good light, and poor publicity really won't help you if this ends up going to court."

"Okay. I'll do my best to avoid anyone with a mic and camera. Any luck finding out who posted my bail?"

"None," the detective said. "I don't know what to tell you. It could be related to the case, or maybe you just have a very good friend somewhere. Oh, before I go, there's one more thing. I asked animal control about that dog, and they said you're free to pick her up if you want to. You shouldn't have any issues—I guess you and Zander were both listed on her vet records."

"That's great news, Detective Jefferson," Moira said with a rush of relief. "Thank you so much. I'll pick her up this evening."

Smiling, she went back inside the antique shop. She had found the perfect wedding dress, and she got to break Flower out of doggy jail. It was turning out to be a pretty good day after all.

CHAPTER EIGHT

Though she was eager to pick up Flower from animal control, she still had one more wedding-related stop to make before the day was over. With her dress safely in the back of the SUV, she drove her friends to a small bakery in the middle of Lake Marion. She had no doubt that they would all enjoy what was waiting for them inside.

"Moira, I'm so glad you could come on such short notice," the older woman who ran the bakery said. She stepped out from around the counter and gave the deli owner a quick hug before introducing herself to her friends. "I'm Fanni Lemming, the owner of Angelic Cake Bakery. I think I've seen at least one of you in here before... yes, you stop in a couple of times a week for scones, don't you?"

"Yeah," Karissa admitted, grinning. "I keep telling myself I should start making my own breakfast, but I just can't get enough of your lemon scones."

"There's no shame in that," Fanni said with a grin. "If you like our scones, then you should love the cake samples I have for you today."

"We're all very eager to try them," Moira assured her. "We've been shopping all morning, and haven't even had lunch yet."

"Great. I'll get Colleen to bring out the samples. Why don't you join me at the table in the back? It will be nice and quiet, and you can take your time going over each flavor."

Picking out the flavor of her wedding cake was something that Moira had been looking forward to for weeks. David wasn't too picky when it came to sweets, so he had given her free rein. With him working extra now to make up for the time he would be gone from his cases during their honeymoon, she had agreed to do the tasting with her friends instead of trying to figure out when he could come along.

"Oh my goodness, I love this strawberry cake," Martha said, taking another bite of the small sample piece on her plate. "I've never had anything like it."

"You loved the vanilla and the lemon cakes, too," Karissa said, chuckling.

"They're *all* good. I've never been to a wedding that actually had good cake, but Moira won't be able to keep me away from this."

The deli owner chuckled, taking a small bite of her

own. The strawberry cake, with white chocolate buttercream frosting *was* good. The cake itself wasn't too sweet, and she knew Fanni had used real strawberries in it. It tasted fresh; perfect for a summer wedding.

Then again, *all* of the flavors she had tasted so far had been good, and she still had three more flavors to try: chocolate, coconut, and mocha. When combined with all of the options for frosting and fillings, plus the fact that she could have a different combination of flavors on each tier, the deli owner knew she was going to be faced with some very difficult choices indeed.

"Here's the double chocolate with cocoa mousse," Fanni said, reappearing with another set of plates with small sample pieces on them. The deli owner tried a bite, and was floored by the decadent flavor. At this rate, how was she ever going to choose? Each bite was better than the last.

"So, what do you think it will be?" the bakery owner asked when they had finally finished tasting the last sample; a light and fluffy coconut-flavored cake. "Or do you want some time to talk it over with the lucky man first?"

"I think I'm going to have to ask him," Moira said. "We can do different flavors for each tier, right?"

"Sure thing. I can do pretty much whatever you want —different-flavored tiers, any size or shape of cake you'd like, fondant, buttercream, or even whipped frosting..."

"Let's stick with the buttercream," the deli owner told her. "Fondant looks nice, but it doesn't taste good, and whipped frosting won't last for long before it starts to wilt. I think buttercream is a nice compromise between them."

"It's nice to talk with someone who knows what she

wants," Fanni said with a chuckle. "Go ahead and take a few days to talk it over. Do you think you could let me know by Monday at the latest?"

"Definitely. I should be able to give you a call tomorrow, in fact. Thanks so much, Fanni."

With their bellies full of sugar, the four woman left the bakery in search of some real food. Feeling nostalgic, Moira suggested Arlo's Diner. The diner had been around for as long as she could remember, and she and Candice had gone there every week when Candice was younger. Run by the same irascible elderly gentleman, the food hadn't changed much at all for over twenty years. It was a blast from the past for Moira and Martha, who had both grown up in Maple Creek.

"I can't believe old Arlo is still running this place. Didn't it come close to closing down a while ago?" Martha asked, idly swirling the last of her fries in ketchup.

"A couple of times," Moira told her. "But he pulls through. I doubt he makes much money off of this place, but he sure loves it. Give me another twenty years at the deli, and I'm sure I'll be just like him."

"David will keep you on your toes," Denise assured her. "Besides, I'm sure you'll hand the deli off to Darrin when the time is right, and enjoy some well-earned retirement."

"Maybe." Moira wrinkled her nose. "I'm not ready to think about all of that yet, though. First I've got to get through the next few weeks without having a breakdown or getting hauled off to jail again. Come on, we should get going. Talking about the deli reminded me—I need to stop there and drop off next week's schedule before going to pick up Flower from animal control."

After saying goodbye to her friends, and thanking

them sincerely for spending the day shopping with her—they really were the best group of bridesmaids she could ask for—she drove over to the deli and popped inside just as Darrin was finishing up a transaction with a customer. Not wanting to interrupt, she dropped the schedule off next to the register and started to head back towards the door.

"Ms. D, wait," Darrin said quickly. "I've got a message for you from someone. Hold on..."

He finished ringing up the customer, then pulled open the drawer beneath the register and pulled out the yellow notepad kept there for just that purpose.

"A kid stopped in a few hours ago and wanted to know when you'd be in again. I told him tomorrow morning, and he said he would stop by. He wanted to know how Hazel was doing."

Moira blinked, stunned. She had long since given up

finding out who Hazel's first owner had been. Nearly a year ago, someone had abandoned the pregnant dog behind the deli with nothing but a note begging the deli owner to take care of her. Why was her original owner choosing now to come looking for her?

"A kid?" she asked.

"Yeah, maybe twelve or thirteen. He rode his bike over, and I didn't see any parents."

"Thanks for telling me, Darrin. I'll have Karissa send me some new pictures of Hazel tonight so he can see that she's happy. I hope he doesn't want her back... Karissa loves that dog, and Hazel is utterly spoiled."

She left the deli with her good mood slightly dampened. It would be wonderful to be able to give the kid good news about his dog, but she couldn't help wondering why he was choosing *now*, nearly a year after leaving her tied up behind the deli, to find out what had happened to her. *Maybe he saw that news story about my arrest and Zander's murder,* she thought, feeling a new rush of anger towards the reporter and whoever had been leaking information about her at the police station. *And now the poor kid thinks he gave his dog to a killer.* Well, come tomorrow, she would set his mind at ease. Hazel was very happy with David's sister, and that would just have to be good enough for the kid.

CHAPTER NINE

"I'm glad Jefferson talked Animal Control into letting you bring her home." David reached down to scratch the little yellow dog's ears. Flower wriggled with joy. She had been ecstatic ever since Moira had picked her up, and her energy showed no sign of fading.

"Me too. She looked so unhappy there. I hated seeing her locked in that cold metal kennel," the deli owner said. She prodded her fork at the salad on her plate. The cherry bourbon dressing was one of her favorites, but she had no appetite. What had happened to her good mood from earlier in the day?

Seeing Flower in that kennel was like being back in jail myself, she thought. *I've been doing my best not to think too much about my arrest, but that's a mistake. If something goes wrong in the investigation, I could end up in prison.*

"Is everything all right?" David asked her. As always, he seemed in tune with her moods. She smiled at him.

"Just thinking," she said. "Sorry. I feel bad for inviting you over for dinner, then just sitting here in silence the whole time."

"Don't worry about it. This is what marriage is about, isn't it? 'For better or for worse,' right? I know you've got a lot on your plate right now, what with both the wedding and Zander's death. I just wish there was more I could do to help."

"Oh, you've been wonderful, David. I'm just a

worrier. Have you managed to find any leads on who might have killed Zander? Just knowing that you had *some* idea of who it could be would help a lot."

"Well…" He hesitated, and she thought she knew why. *He thinks if he tells me, I'll go off and try to investigate myself.*

"Please? I promise not to do anything reckless."

"I did find something that raised a red flag for me," he relented. "Someone named Danehill approached Zander with an impressive offer on his land a few months ago. Yesterday, he approached Zander's aunt —she's his closest living relative, and his estate went to her since he died without a will—and made another offer."

Moira gave a low whistle. "You think this guy wanted Zander's property badly enough to kill him? How did you find all of this out?"

"I'll tell you if you promise to keep in confidential."

She nodded. "Of course."

"His aunt approached me right after the offer was made and hired me to look into it. She thought it seemed pretty suspicious too—suspicious enough to warrant putting a private investigator on Danehill's tail."

"Have you told any of this to the police yet?" she asked hopefully. Maybe Zander's murder would be solved sooner than she had hoped. Then he could finally rest in peace... and she could rest without worrying about trying to run the deli from prison.

"I gave them the information about the offers on Zander's property as soon as I found out," he told her. "I want this solved by our wedding."

"Me too," she told him, picking up her fork again. Knowing that David and the police had at least one other suspect made her feel a lot better. In no time at all, her name would be cleared, her wedding would be over, and she would be looking forward to a happy life with the man sitting across the table from her.

The next morning was a hectic rush. With three dogs, it took her longer than usual to get everyone fed, put out, and settled in for the day. Even after they had been taken care of, they were underfoot the entire time that she was trying to get ready. Moira didn't quite trust Flower—used to roaming outside on the farm—alone in the house, so she had to be gated in the mud room—which meant finding the baby gate and rushing to set out a dog bed and water dish for the energetic pup. Flower had decided that the entire morning routine was the most exciting thing that she had ever experienced.

A spilled mug of coffee and subsequent change of clothes later, Moira was finally ready to head out. At the last minute, thinking of the kid who was supposed to be stopping in at the deli sometime that morning, she snapped a picture of Flower. If their positions had been reversed, she knew that she would love to see pictures of the puppies.

"Hey, Dante. It smells wonderful in here."

It was a phrase that she found herself saying every morning that the young man was responsible for opening the shop. A good cook all around, he had a real gift for quiches. The mini quiches had been his idea, in fact. A large part of the success of the deli's breakfast hours was due to his cooking.

"Thanks, Ms. D. I tried a new recipe today—parsley and sun-dried tomatoes with shredded mozzarella on top. The first batch should be done in just a few minutes."

"Will you set a couple aside on a plate for me?" she asked. "I've got to get started on the pot roast stew. It's going to take hours to cook, and I don't want to leave our lunch guests waiting."

"Sure thing. I'll grab a cup of coffee for you, too."

"Dante, you are amazing."

Moira washed her hands, pulled out the slow cooker and a frying pan, and got to work. With a loud sizzle she put the pot roast in the pan and began the process of browning it on all sides. Even before she seasoned it, the juicy cut of meat smelled amazing as it began to cook. Today's soup was going to be a real treat, that was certain.

Once she finished browning the roast, she put it in the slow cooker and began the task of chopping up carrots, celery, onions, and fresh garlic. After dumping the pile of veggies into the cooker as well, she turned her attention to the all-important seasonings.

Salt and pepper were a necessity of course, but she also added a bit of Worcestershire sauce to give the roast even more flavor. For fresh herbs, she decided to go with rosemary, basil, and oregano. Last but not least, she added just enough beef broth to partially cover the roast. Once the meat was done cooking, she would pull it apart and add more broth to turn the pot roast into a delicious and hearty stew.

"I'm definitely not going to be losing any weight today," she said as she put the glass top on the slow cooker. "Between quiches for breakfast, this pot roast stew for lunch, and whatever I end up grabbing for dinner, I might even gain a few pounds."

"No worries, Ms. D. Our food isn't that unhealthy," Dante replied. "It's all cooked here, so at least you know what's in it. I can hardly eat anymore at big chain restaurants that start with frozen food."

"There is something to be said for knowing where your food comes from and what's in it," Moira agreed. She thought of Zander, and how passionate he had been about farming and being involved with the community, and felt a rush of despair. Not only had she lost a friend, but he had also been one of her most trusted sources for fresh produce. What would happen to everything he had built now?

Once the deli had officially opened for the morning, Moira spent most of her time hovering around the cash register, waiting for the mysterious kid that had missed her yesterday to return. It wasn't until nearly noon when he finally showed up. Her shift almost over, the deli owner had ducked back into the kitchen to look through her mail when Dante poked his head through the kitchen doors to tell her that there was someone there to see her.

The kid's age was impossible to tell. He could have been anywhere from twelve to fourteen, and was sorely in need of a haircut. But when he approached the register, she knew right away that he was the one.

"Are you Mrs. Darling?" he asked.

"Well, I'm not married, but yes. You stopped in yesterday about Hazel?"

He nodded. "I'm Adam. She was my dog, and I just wanted to know how she was doing. Did you keep her? Did she have her puppies?"

"She had six wonderful, healthy puppies. I didn't keep her myself, but my fiancé's sister took her. She's very happy and spoiled now."

"That's good." Adam beamed. "I know you probably don't want me to, but is there any way I could see her one more time? I miss her, and she probably misses me too."

"Well... I'll see. I'll have to ask the lady who owns her now, okay? If you don't mind me asking, why are you asking about her after all this time? It's been almost a year."

"I didn't want to before, in case my dad saw me hanging around here. I told him that she ran away, and he'd be mad if he found out I was lying. He wasn't a very good guy, but he's gone so now I don't have to worry about it."

"Oh... I'm sorry." The deli owner wasn't quite sure what to say. A parent leaving was never a good thing... was it?

"It's 'kay," the kid said with a shrug. "My mom got a new job, and we moved into town, and she even said I could get another dog if I want, as long as it's fixed

PATTI BENNING

this time. I thought I'd see if you wanted to keep Hazel. But if she's happy, I don't want to take her away."

"She is happy, but I'm sure it would be okay if you visited her." An idea was beginning to form in Moira's mind. Adam was looking for a dog... and Flower was looking for a home. It was too good of a coincidence to ignore, but before mentioning anything to the kid, she knew that she needed to check with his mother. "Where does your mom work, Adam? I'd love to stop by and talk to her about something."

"Oh, she runs D's Donuts. It's right down the street, you can almost see it from here."

"I know where it is," she said with a smile. The donut shop had opened up a few weeks ago, wafting tantalizing smells down the street. Although she hadn't stopped in yet, she had been meaning to. "I'll talk to my friend about setting up a time for you to

104

see Hazel, then I'll stop by the donut shop and talk to your mom, okay?"

The kid nodded, seemingly pleased with this plan. The deli owner was surprised but glad that she had finally found out who Hazel's old owner was—she just hoped that Adam and his mother didn't complicate matters. Karissa would not be happy if they tried to take her dog from her.

CHAPTER TEN

After getting the go-ahead from Karissa, Moira made good on her word and stopped at the donut shop on her way home from work. It was an interesting place; the sign, in sprawling cursive letters, welcomed her to D's Donuts. When she stepped through the doors, she noticed a scattering of arcade machines to her left. Several teenagers were playing at the machines. On the other side of the store were a few tables, the register, and a large, well-lit display of donuts.

"Hi, welcome to D's Donuts. Can I help you?" the teen working at the counter asked as she approached.

"Um, yes. I'm looking for... Adam's mom." She didn't know his mom's name, something that she wished she had realized before. Hopefully this girl knew who she was talking about.

"Oh, Robyn? She's in the back. Hold on a sec."

The girl slipped through a swinging door and reappeared a moment later with a middle-aged woman in tow.

"Did Adam do something?" she asked nervously, wiping her the flour on her hands onto the apron that she was wearing. "Is he in trouble?"

"No, no, nothing like that. I don't know if you know... but he left his dog behind my deli last year."

The woman winced. "It sounds terrible when you say it like that. I told him he should take her to the pound, but he was worried they would put the puppies down. I guess one of his friends saw your dogs at the fair last year, and he got it into his mind that you were the perfect person for Hazel. I was going to send her away to someone who rescues dogs, but he snuck her out before I could do anything. His father was a real piece of work. I don't think he'd actually have hurt the dog, but Adam took his threats seriously. You can't fault him for trying to protect her. He loved Hazel."

"I gathered some of that from what he told me, but it's nice to hear the full story. I've been wondering about it since I took her in. Like I told Adam, she got adopted by a friend of mine and is very happy and spoiled," Moira told her.

"That's good news. I told him that she would probably be settled in with her new owners, but he still wanted to check."

"That's actually what I wanted to talk to you about... he mentioned you said he could get another dog?"

The other woman nodded. "He was half-hoping to get Hazel back, but I'm sure he'll understand that she's happy and her new owner doesn't want to give her up. He's a good kid, he'll want what's best for her."

"He seemed fine with that, but I actually had another idea. I have one of Hazel's puppies at my house right now. She just lost her owner, so I was thinking, if she and Adam get along and it was okay with you... maybe he could take Flower? Obviously it wouldn't be the same as him getting Hazel herself back, but it would be a great solution all around. She's a very sweet, happy dog."

"Flower... that's a pretty name." Robyn smiled. "I think that's a wonderful idea. What did he say?"

"I haven't mentioned it to him yet—I wanted to run it by you first. The friend of mine that ended up adopting Hazel said she'd be happy to let them get together and see each other, so I thought if it was okay with you we could find a time to let him see Hazel and meet Flower all at once. Here, I'll leave you my number, and you can call me after you talk it over with him."

"Thanks so much. You didn't have to do any of this."

"I'm just glad that I was able to help. Hazel is a wonderful dog, and Adam seems like a nice kid." Moira smiled at the other woman. "This is a neat place that you have here. I bet once school starts, a lot of kids will stop in after class. Do you own this place? What does the D in the store's name stand for?"

"I just manage the store, it's a franchise," Robyn said with a chuckle. "I wish I owned it—I'd be rich! The D stands for the owner's name, Danehill. I guess he thought 'Danehill's Donuts' just didn't have quite the same ring to it."

The rest of their conversation went by in a blur to Moira. She did her best to act as normally as she could, but inside she was reeling. Danehill—that was the name of the person that had tried to buy Zander's farm twice. Did David know that he owned a donut franchise? What on earth could Danehill want Zander's property for? What would the donut man be willing to kill for?

Itching to talk to David, she invited him over to her house for an impromptu dinner. She didn't mention anything about the case to him; she had discovered long ago that it was easier to get him to talk if she caught him unawares with her questions. She would just slip the subject of Danehill in between talk of their wedding and plans for their honeymoon.

First, though, she needed to figure out what she was going to make for dinner. A quick call to the deli

solved that; she asked Allison, who had the afternoon shift, to put aside a couple of servings of the
pot roast stew for her. Paired with some of the delicious bread from the deli and a fresh salad, it would
make for a hearty meal—and best of all, she
wouldn't have to take any extra time out of her day
for cooking. She had plenty of time to run her
errands before swinging by the deli in the evening
and picking up a nice warm meal to bring home to
David. *Sometimes things work out perfectly*, she
thought. *Too bad it never seems to happen with the
big stuff.*

CHAPTER ELEVEN

She had planned just to swing by the deli for the food and then hurry home to get everything prepared for David, but when she saw the refrigerated truck parked in the alley around back, she decided to stay for a little bit and help Cameron and Jenny unload. Even though they had been working for her for months, she still didn't feel that she knew them as well as the others. Since they were responsible for most of the catering jobs, they didn't spend anywhere near as much time at the deli itself as everyone else did. Still, they were part of the crew, and it never hurt to spend some extra time with her employees.

"Hey Jenny, how did the job go?" she asked, setting

down her purse next to the big take-home container
of soup that Allison had waiting for her.

"It went well, Ms. D. Shelby was happy with everything, and she even said to tell you that she was
planning on hiring the deli to cater her other daughter's open house this fall."

"That's what I love to hear," said Moira with a smile.
"You and Cameron have been doing great here. I'm
so glad I hired you."

"Thanks. I love this job, I really do."

The deli owner watched as the young woman
walked away, noting that she still seemed unusually
subdued. *She must really be taking Zander's death hard*,
Moira thought. *I wonder if Cameron has noticed?* She
knew that the red-haired young man was smitten
with Jenny, but wasn't sure how much they really
hung out outside of work.

She got her chance to ask him soon enough. He was out in the refrigerated truck, taking inventory to make sure nothing was missing.

"Hey," she said, stepping up into the truck. She hadn't once regretted buying it—the ability to transport their own food without renting a vehicle was wonderful, and she had been able to lower their catering prices too, once the truck had been paid off. "I heard the open house went well. Congratulations on another job well done."

"It was a piece of cake," he said with a grin. "I love open houses. People are just there to have fun and eat some good food. It's not like a wedding, where everyone's emotions are running high."

"You know you don't have to work during my reception if you don't want to—"

"Oh, I didn't mean it like that, Ms. D. I'm looking forward to your wedding."

Cameron, Jenny, and Allison had all volunteered to work at Moira's wedding reception as caterers for free as a wedding gift to her. Though she would still be paying for the food, of course, having the deli cater her own reception was saving her a lot of money.

"I just feel bad that the three of you are going to be doing so much work," she said. "But thank you. Not having to find a caterer makes things so much easier for me."

"And hey, at least you know you're going to get good food," he added.

"That's true. I couldn't ask for anything better." She hesitated, glancing back towards the deli to make sure Jenny, who had taken a box of dirty tablecloths in to be washed, was still inside. "I've been wanting to ask you... do you think Jenny's doing all right? You spend the most time with her out of all of us."

"You mean Zander? She's taking it pretty rough. To be honest, I don't know what she saw in the guy."

"You didn't like him?"

"He was too old for her." He shrugged, and changed the subject. "Any luck tracking down the person that paid your bail?"

"Not a single clue, as far as I know," she told him. "It's a real mystery. I don't think I even *know* someone with that much money lying around."

"I'm sure you'll find out eventually." He gave her a quick smile. "Oh, did we leave you enough soup?

Allison was concerned that we should have left more."

"It looks like enough—it just needs to feed David and me. Which reminds me, I should probably get going. It was good to catch up, Cameron. Keep up the good work. I'll see you later."

With that she climbed out of the food truck and hurried back inside. Somehow the time had gotten away from her, and if she didn't hurry, she was going to be late.

"This looks amazing," David said, sitting down at the table across from her. "Doubly so, since I didn't have time for lunch."

"Thanks. It's just leftovers from the deli. I didn't have time to make something fresh."

"It looks perfectly good to me." He glanced to the side, where Maverick, Keeva, and Flower were lined up, each dog watching them closely. "The dogs definitely seem interested."

"I haven't fed them dinner yet," she admitted. "I barely got back in time to heat the soup up and throw the salad together before you got here. It was a busy day. I'll tell you about it while we eat."

She filled David in on what had happened with Adam, picking at her salad between sentences. He was surprised that Hazel's former owner had gotten into contact with her after all this time.

"I do think that your idea to give him Flower is a good one," he said. "As long as they like each other and they seem like a good family. From what you said it sounds like they are, even though they were in a bad situation before."

"It seems like a good solution for everyone," she said. "But... there is something else that I'm worried about."

"What is it?" he asked, concerned.

"Robyn, Adam's mom... while I was talking to her I found out who owns the donut shop. It's Mr. Danehill."

David put his spoon down, frowning. "That's... interesting. I ran a background check on him, but hadn't gotten results back yet. I know that he runs a corporation called Danehill, LLC, but haven't been able to get a line on what they actually do. The company seems to have links with a lot of different industries."

"I was thinking... well, Robyn seemed nice enough —maybe next time I see her, I could ask her some questions about her boss? I don't know how involved in the donut shop he is, but she might have over-heard something important."

"Moira, you know I don't want you getting involved—"

"I'm not getting involved, though. I'd just be asking a fellow mom some questions while her kid plays with Hazel and Flower. There's nothing suspicious about that."

The private investigator eyed her closely. "All right," he said at last. "I suppose I wouldn't be able to stop you anyway. Just... be careful about what you say, okay? If Danehill did kill Zander, we don't want it getting back to him that we're onto him."

"I'll be careful," she promised. "The last thing I want is for this case to get even more complicated. My freedom's on the line, after all.""

CHAPTER TWELVE

The day of the meeting with Adam, Hazel, and Flower started off strangely and only got weirder. Certain that she had scheduled herself to work at the deli that morning, she got up bright and early and got herself out the door with time to spare. Usually on the days that she worked mornings, she had the first thirty minutes to herself as she prepared the quiches and breakfast cookies, since whatever employee was working with her that day wouldn't arrive until minutes before the deli actually opened. Today, however, she was surprised to see two cars already parked in front of the little shop.

Walking inside to find Allison and Cameron busily preparing for the day she said, "You two are here early. Cameron, I didn't even think you were sched-uled to work today. Don't you and Jenny have that retirement party to cater tomorrow evening?"

"We're on the schedule, Ms. D. See?" Allison said. She held out the paper, and Moira scrutinized it with a slight frown. Sure enough, Allison and Cameron's names were down for this shift... but she could have sworn that she hadn't scheduled them.

"Well... I guess you're right." Her frown deepened when she saw black smudges on the tips of Cameron's fingers. "What happened? That looks almost like fingerprint ink."

In fact, his fingers looked exactly like hers had after she had been fingerprinted during her arrest. The Maple Creek police station had yet to upgrade to electric fingerprinting equipment.

"Yeah, I got brought in last night," he said, rubbing

his fingers self-consciously. "I guess they thought I may have had some sort of connection with Zander. They brought Jenny in too, and asked her some questions. They must be getting pretty desperate. I hardly knew the guy."

"What sorts of things did they ask her?"

He shrugged. "No idea. She left before they finished with me."

Odder and odder, the deli owner thought. *Why are the police questioning my employees now? Did they hit a dead end with Danehill?*

"So I guess you have the day off, huh, Ms. D?" said Allison, jolting her out of her thoughts.

"I suppose so," Moira said slowly. She looked back and forth between her employees, getting the

127

nagging feeling that she was missing something, but both of them just smiled at her. "I guess I'll get going, then. I'll see you two later."

She left the deli, walking slowly back to her car as she tried to puzzle out what had just happened. She was *certain* that she had been supposed to work today. *Maybe I'm losing it* she thought. Her wedding was, after all, in just over a week.

As soon as she slid into her car, her cell phone started ringing. She jumped slightly, then dug it out of her purse. The caller ID told her it was Karissa.

"Hey, something came up for me later today. Do you think we could get the dogs together sooner? Like, maybe in an hour or so? I already talked to Robyn and she said it was fine."

"Yeah, I suppose so," Moira said. "It's weird, I thought I was supposed to go in to work this morning, but apparently I scheduled myself the entire day off."

"That works out pretty well, then, doesn't it? I'll see ya soon! I think Hazel knows something different is about to happen—she seems excited."

With that, her friend hung up, and Moira was left even more confused. What on earth was happening this morning?

After swinging by her house to get Flower, who was ecstatic to be going for a ride, she drove straight over to Lake Marion and Karissa's apartment. David's sister waved her and Flower inside. The sight of Hazel and her daughter meeting each other for the first time in months brought a smile to Moira's face. She could see the exact moment when the two dogs recognized each other. They both exploded into a flurry of wagging tails and licking tongues. The two women had barely gotten them to calm down when there was a knock at the door and Adam and Robyn walked in.

Hazel must have been having the best day of her life; she recognized Adam right off that bat and was so excited to see him that she nearly knocked him over. The boy laughed and sat down on the floor while the dog rubbed her face against his head.

"Look at that," Robyn said with a teary smile. "She remembers him."

They let the lab and the boy reconnect for a few minutes, then Karissa called Hazel over and let Flower go forward. The younger dog approached Adam with her usual enthusiasm, and soon the two of them were playing as if they had known each other forever.

"They seem like a match made in heaven," Moira said. "What do you think, Robyn?"

"As long as she's relatively well behaved, I'd love to tell him he can have her. What did you say happened to her owner, again?"

"He was killed," the deli owner explained in a low voice, not wanting the boy to hear. "I'm not sure if you've seen anything on the news, but her owner was Zander Marsh."

"How horrible. It's odd, the name is familiar, but I don't think I heard it through the news... did he own a farm a bit of a way out of town?"

"He did," Moira said. "Did you know him?"

"Not me, no, but my boss did. If it's the guy I'm thinking of, Mr. Danehill was talking about wanting to buy some land from him."

"What would he want with a hunk of farmland?"

"Oh, he wants to open a factory where he can make donuts and other snacks in bulk to ship around the country. I guess Zander's land was zoned right for industrial use or something. I don't know much about it."

Mental gears turning, Moira bit her lip. She wanted to ask more questions, but remembered her promise to David to be careful. She didn't want to risk Robyn letting something slip to Danehill. If he had killed Zander, the last thing she wanted was for him to find out that she was on to him.

"Can I keep her?" Adam asked, grinning up at them as Flower dropped a squeaky toy into his lap.

Moira smiled at him. "If it's okay with your mom, she's yours."

Saying goodbye to Flower for the second time was bittersweet. She was sure she would see the dog again—she could already tell that Robyn was someone she could easily be friends with, and Adam and Karissa were already making plans to get Hazel and her daughter together for playdates. Flower, as usual, was overjoyed at the chance to jump into someone else's car and go on another ride. Moira had no doubts that the dog would be happy, but it was still hard to see her go.

"Take good care of her," she said.

"I will!" Adam promised. "She'll be my very best friend."

She and Karissa waved as Robyn and her son drove away with Flower in the back of their car, then turned to head back inside the apartment once the two were out of sight.

"I should get out of your hair," Moira said. "The rest of my day is unexpectedly clear. I'll probably call Martha and go over the wedding plans again."

"You're not going anywhere," Karissa said, her face breaking into a grin. "We worked too hard to plan this."

"What are you talking about?"

"Why, your bachelorette party, of course. What sort of bridesmaids would we be if we didn't throw you one? Martha and Denise will be here soon. Candice is going to go over to your house and take care of the dogs, and David knows not to worry if you don't answer your phone. All you have to do is relax, have fun, and enjoy everything we have planned."

CHAPTER THIRTEEN

Moira was still stunned half an hour later when she and her friends all piled into Denise's car.

"I don't understand how you managed all of this," she said. "You ladies are amazing."

"It took a bit of work," Martha admitted. "We had to convince Allison and Cameron to fudge the schedule. That was really the hardest part. We had to promise them that you wouldn't be mad."

"Allison texted Karissa right after you let the deli. We

needed to catch you before you made different plans. Even Robyn was in on it."

"Wow." The deli owner shook her head. "This is more than I deserve."

"We haven't even started yet," Karissa said with a grin. "We have a whole day planned out. First stop is the spa."

What followed was probably the most relaxing day that Moira had ever had. They drove down to Traverse City and spent hours in a spa, all four of them getting massages, mani-pedis, and facial treatments. The deli owner felt the stress of the last few weeks completely melt away.

After the spa, the four women spent a few hours shopping in town. Martha was the only one who got down to Traverse City on a regular basis; the others usually made do with the small shops and boutiques nearer to Maple Creek. Moira was pleased to find a beautiful new dress, and the perfect shoes to go with her wedding dress.

By the time they were done shopping, the deli owner was beginning to feel hungry. She was about to suggest that they stop somewhere to eat, when Denise made a sharp turn into a parking lot.

"Here we are," she said. "Our final stop—the Melting Bowl."

Moira had never been to the restaurant before, but judging from the delicious scent when they entered, the food here would be scrumptious.

"We reserved a private room," Martha explained as Karissa gave the hostess her name. "I've come here a few times for work, and I think you'll like it. They mostly do fondue, and their food is absolutely amazing. Plus, it's fun to do it yourself."

The deli owner got another surprise when they entered their room. Banners and decorations hung from the walls congratulating the bride-to-be, and her grinning friends put a sash over her head.

"We've got music, food, and wine," Denise said. "As much of all of it as you could want. We thought you might like this better than going to a club."

"Definitely," Moira said. "You guys, this is beyond anything I could even imagine. You didn't have to do all of this for me."

"Of course we did," Martha said. "You'd do the same for any of us, after all, and we know it."

It was late when they finally returned to Maple Creek. Moira was full and sleepy, but brimming over with happiness. Not much could beat a day out with friends. The bachelorette party had somehow managed to drive home the fact that in a week, she would be a married woman. It was a wonderful thought; as far as she was concerned, the wedding couldn't arrive quickly enough.

"Thank you so much," she said when they got to Karissa's apartment. "I had a wonderful time. It was a perfect day, and it meant the world to me."

"I'm glad you enjoyed it, Moira," said Martha. "You definitely deserved it."

She gave each of her friends a quick, thankful hug goodbye before sliding into her own vehicle and starting the engine. She hoped to be in bed within the hour with a cup of tea, a good book, and the dogs beside her. The perfect end to the day, as far as she was concerned.

Moira slept late the next morning, relishing the

PATTI BENNING

memories of the day before, and giddy at the thought that she was another day closer to marrying David. *And after the wedding, we leave for our honeymoon!* They had finally decided on a destination; rather, they hadn't been able to decide on *one* destination, and instead had opted for a tour of Europe. Before she knew it, she would be journeying across France, Spain, and Italy with her new husband.

Thoughts of the honeymoon quickly brought along with them the dark reminder of the pending murder charges against her. They hadn't bought tickets or set more than tentative dates for the trip yet, since she wouldn't be able to leave the state while she was out on bail.

"I want this mess to be over," she groaned, sitting up in bed. "I just want to clear my name and get married. Is that too much to ask?"

What she saw when she drove up to the deli that afternoon brought her mood even lower. The

Beyond News van was sitting in the parking lot again and Brendan, the reporter, was leaning casually against it talking to a woman that Moira didn't recognize.

"What's going on?" she asked, striding up to them after she parked.

"Ah, Ms. Darling, just the woman I wanted to see. You never called about that interview you promised. You must have lost my card. Is now a good time to talk?"

"No," she said shortly. "Who are you?" This last was to the woman that he had been talking to.

"I'm Emily-Ann," she said. "A *former* customer of yours. I don't give money to murderers."

Moira gaped as the still-unfamiliar woman spun on

her heel and stalked away. Turning to Brendan, she said, "What on earth are you doing? You can't come here and chase my customers away like this."

"I was just telling her the facts," he said, spreading his hands in a gesture of innocence. "I'd love to get *your* side of the story, of course. Maybe then I'd have something else to tell people."

She glared at him, feeling trapped and hating it. What could she do, though? She couldn't afford the bad publicity that he was spreading about her. Maybe an interview *would* help.

"Fine," she said at last. "Come on in. I don't have long, though, all right?"

"Of course. We'll be out of your hair like *that.*" He snapped his fingers, then waved his cameraman forward. "This is Rodney, by the way. He'll be filming. Just ignore him."

Brendan followed her inside, then arranged her at one of the corner bistro tables. Moira waved back Darrin and Cameron, who had both approached her with concerned looks on their faces. It seemed to take him ages to be happy with the camera angle, but at last he gave Rodney a thumbs up, and Moira saw a red light on the front of the camera blink to life.

"I'm Brendan Anaheim with Beyond News, and I'm joined today by Moira Darling," he began, facing the camera. She listened in mute silence while he gave the camera a quick run-down of her story. She winced at the parts that made her sound guilty, but she couldn't deny that everything he said was a fact. Moira felt a flare of anger towards whoever the leak at the police station was. They had no right to give out information that was supposed to be secret, like the fact that her fingerprints had been found on the gun.

"We're here today to see if we can solve what may be the biggest mystery of the case so far," he continued. "Moira, can you tell us *who* exactly posted your $60,000 bail?"

"I don't know," she told him, doing her best not to look at the camera. "I was, um, hoping that we could talk about some of the accusations against me, actually. I want people to know that I'm innocent."

"I think what the public is the most curious about is your bail," he said. "Your mysterious benefactor has made this tale unexpectedly spicy. Aren't you getting married pretty soon?"

"I am, but—"

"Is that why you're reluctant to give out the name of the person that paid your bail? Is he an old flame, maybe? Someone you've been having a secret affair with?"

"Oh, this is ridiculous," Cameron said. Moira didn't know who was more surprised at his outburst—her or the reporter.

"Do you have some juicy details?" Brendan asked, swiveling to thrust the microphone into her employee's face.

"Yes. I paid it. Happy? Ms. D's a good boss, and I didn't like the thought of her sitting in jail."

Cameron refused to answer any more questions. Darrin helped him shoo the reporter and cameraman out of the restaurant, then they both returned to Moira, who was gaping at her red-haired employee.

"What? How? You don't have that kind of money. I know I don't pay you *that* much."

Cameron sighed. "Look, I didn't want this to get out... but I've got money. A lot of it. I come from a wealthy family, and it makes a lot of things easier, but it wasn't something I wanted everyone here to know. Especially not Jenny."

"If you've got that sort of money, then why on earth are you working for me?" Moira asked. "And why on earth wouldn't you tell Jenny? It's obvious to everyone how you feel about her."

"To answer your first question, I like working here. I've always enjoyed working with food, but I hate the high-stress environment of the big restaurants. Working as a caterer here is fun... but to be honest, I only decided to take the job after I saw that Jenny was working here. It was love at first sight, for me at least," he admitted. "And that leads to your second question. I didn't want her to find out about my money because... well, if I started dating her, I wanted to know it was real. I'd want to know that she actually liked *me*, not just my money. Of course, that plan seems to have backfired. She hardly gives me a second glance."

The deli owner stared at him for a long moment, then slowly shook her head. "David and I have spent hours trying to figure out who would have posted bail for me. I can't believe it was you all along. Thank you."

"It's the least I could do," he told her. "Even just working here for half a year, I've been able to see everything that you do for your employees. I figured it wouldn't hurt to help you out a bit. Sorry it caused so much trouble—maybe I should have just come clean then, but I still had my hopes that I'd be able to win Jenny over with my personality instead of my bank account." He sighed. "I guess the cat's out of the bag now."

"Not necessarily," Moira said after a moment's thought. "Beyond News isn't exactly a huge station.

Brendan himself said that they were 'up and coming,' and I get the feeling that this is the first really big story that he's covered. There's a good chance that Jenny won't see his broadcast."

"I hope you're right," he said.

The deli owner shook her head again, grinning. "I guess you didn't really need that raise I gave you, huh?"

CHAPTER FOURTEEN

Moira promised Cameron that she wouldn't mention his secret to Jenny, but she had made no such promises about telling anyone else. Candice and David were both floored at the news.

"I wish he had told us right off the bat," David said. "It would have saved me a lot of fruitless work trying to find out who posted your bail."

"I can understand why he didn't want anyone to know," Moira said. "I do think of him differently now, even though I try to act the same as ever towards him."

"Still, it would have been nice to know."

Moira had half-expected Cameron's revelation to lead to more headway in the case. With one mystery solved, shouldn't that make it all the easier to solve the other? But the days kept passing without more leads, at least, none that she or David could find. Neither of them had any idea what to police were doing, and when Moira called Detective Jefferson, he simply gave her the same tired answer as always. "I'm working on it, Moira. I'll let you know when I have something new."

At last, almost before she knew it, the evening before her wedding had arrived. Her belly felt full of butterflies as she stared at herself in the mirror. Tonight would be her last dinner with David before they were married. The next time they ate together would be at their reception, as husband and wife. The thought sent a thrill through her.

This is also going to be the last night I spend without

him, she thought. *Tomorrow night, we'll be sharing a bed.* That sent a different kind of thrill through her, and she blushed.

Closing her eyes, she tried to calm her nerves. Tomorrow was going to be the happiest day of her life, but also, in a way, the most terrifying. This was a huge step that she was about to take. Tomorrow would be the first day of the rest of her life... but tonight would be a wonderful reminder of the past eighteen months.

They had arranged their last dinner together as an unmarried couple at the Redwood Grill—the site of their first real date, and many dates since. She was wearing one of her very favorite black dresses, a comfortable pair of flats, and simple makeup. Tomorrow she was going to be spending most of her time completely done up, and she was determined to take her comfort when she could.

"Don't be nervous," she whispered to herself. "It's just a date like any other. You've got this."

After the date, she wouldn't see David again until she was walking down the aisle. Candice and Martha, her two maids of honor, were spending the night at her house tonight, and bright and early tomorrow morning they would begin the arduous project of getting her—and themselves—ready for the ceremony. Moira's one comfort was that everything was out of her hands now. All of the arrangements for the wedding had been made, and most were supervised by people whom she trusted deeply. As long as nothing unforeseen came up, all she would have to worry about was not falling on her face while she was trying to match her step to the bridal march.

At the sound of tires on the gravel driveway she straightened up and gave each of the dogs a quick pet goodbye. "Maverick, Keeva, you two be good, all right? Candice should be here soon, and I'll be back in a few hours."

She left them inside and met David just outside her front door. He took her in his arms, then kissed her before uttering a word.

"Ready?" he asked.

She nodded, trying to quell the newest swarm of butterflies in her stomach. *Just another date*, she reminded herself. "Let's go."

Their regular table was waiting for them at the Grill, but Denise had gone the extra mile and had dressed it up with candles and roses. Moira smiled at the sight. She really did have great friends.

"So," he said, sitting down across from her. "How was your day?"

"Busy," she admitted. "There were a lot of last-minute arrangements to make, but at least everything is done now. I'm glad I made a checklist. Whenever I worry that I forgot something, all I have to do is look at the list."

"I wish you'd let me help more," he said. "I feel bad that you've had to do so much by yourself."

"You've been working on the case," she pointed out. "That's just as important. Being married to someone in prison wouldn't be much fun."

"That's true, I suppose." He gazed at her for a moment, then added, "You're beautiful."

"This is one of my favorite dresses for a reason," she joked.

"I don't mean just tonight," he said, taking her hand. "I mean always. You're the most beautiful, the strongest, the most good-hearted person I know.

Every day I feel lucky that you agreed to spend the rest of your life with me."

"That's—" She cleared her throat. "Thank you. I don't even know what to say. I'm the one that's lucky. Before I met you, I hadn't even thought about getting married again."

As they spoke, her nerves melted away. What had she even been nervous about? This was David. Yes, tomorrow would change both of their lives forever, but in the end he was still the same man that she had spent the last year and a half falling deeper and deeper in love with.

"Any news about the case?" she asked an hour later as they were finishing up some of the best pecan pie she had ever tasted.

"Yes, but unfortunately nothing good," he said. "I finally tracked down some information about Danehill. He couldn't have killed Zander. He's been in Canada since before the murder."

"So we're back to having no idea who did it?" she asked, disappointed.

"I'm sure something will turn up," David told her. "Let's not worry about all of that now. I don't want it to distract from our wedding."

"All right," she agreed, trying to push her concern to the back of her mind. "I don't want anything to distract from the wedding either. I want it to be perfect."

When he drove her home that evening, his good-night kiss lingered. She wanted the moment to last forever, but eventually he pulled away.

"See you tomorrow," he said softly, grinning. "I love you."

She could hardly contain her own smile as she let herself indoors. She knew that tomorrow would be a hectic, crazy, wonderful day, and afterwards they would have the murder charges against her still looming, but right now, in that moment, there wasn't a single thing to worry about.

CHAPTER FIFTEEN

"Just breathe out, Moira. I can't get it tight if you don't. Quit hyperventilating."

Focusing on her breathing, Moira consciously slowed it down and exhaled deeply. Martha took the opportunity to pull the laces tight and tie them off.

"What do you think?"

The deli owner turned to the full-length mirror and gazed at herself. Her hair and makeup hadn't been done yet out of fear of smudging something while she got dressed, but even so, she looked trans-formed. The dress was just as beautiful as she remembered, and she couldn't wait for David to see her in it.

"It's perfect. Thank you, Martha. I can't even imagine trying to put this thing on alone."

"You'd have to be a contortionist," her friend agreed.

"Mom, the hair lady is here," Candice called from the doorway. Moira looked up in time to see the cosmetologist stride in. She winced. Freya was supposed to be great, but the deli owner had never enjoyed having others do her hair and makeup for her. The thought of sitting still for the next hour while someone poked and prodded at her wasn't a tempting one, but there was no getting around it.

"Take a seat right over there," the woman directed.

"Are you sticking with the plan that we went over before? Hair down, semi-natural makeup?"

"Yes, if you can. Thank you."

She took her seat and tried to relax as the woman pinned a protective sheer around her neck to protect her dress from the hair spray and makeup. This would be over soon enough, and then the wedding would begin.

Freya had nearly finished when a knock sounded at the door of the dressing area that the church had let them use. Martha frowned, checked her watch, then went to answer it. Moira, who had been forbidden to move her head, kept her eyes on the mirror in an effort to figure out who it was. She was surprised to see Jenny walk in. The young brunette looked nervous, but she had a certain determination to her face. It was the deli owner's turn to frown. Had something gone wrong with the food for the reception?

"Can I talk to you?" the young woman asked quietly. "Alone?" Her eyes darted anxiously between the others.

"She's not done yet," Freya told her with a frown. "You'll have to wait."

"Please, Ms. D. It's important."

Moira met her employee's eyes and read the urgency there. Whatever was going on, she knew it couldn't wait, or Jenny wouldn't have interrupted.

"All right," she said. "Sorry, Freya. I'm going to have to step into the hallway really quickly."

Ignoring her hairdresser's annoyed sigh, she shrugged out of the sheet and got up. A quick glance in the mirror tempted her to stay and take a longer look—could that beautiful woman really be her? But Jenny was fidgeting at her side, and she knew there was no time to spare.

"What is it?" she asked the young woman when they reached the privacy of the hall. "Did something happen?"

"It's about Cam," Jenny whispered.

So she found out about his money, Moira thought with a sigh. She could understand the other woman's need to talk to someone, but found herself wishing that Jenny had waited until the reception at least. *I need to be ready in time for the ceremony.*

"He didn't want—"

"I think he killed Zander."

The deli owner choked on her words, completely floored by what the other woman had said. "What? Why on earth would you think *that*?"

"The police..." Jenny took a deep breath. "They brought me in and asked me a lot of questions about him."

"What sort of questions?"

"Stuff like how well he knew Zander, and if he knew that we were dating, and if I knew where he was the morning of the murder."

"I'm sure they were just covering all of their bases," the deli owner said. "They *arrested* me, remember? And I know I didn't do it."

"But that's not all." Jenny bit her lip. "This morning, I had the news on while I was getting ready. It was that same station as before, Beyond News or whatever, and they said that according to Zander's calendar, he had met with Cam the night before he died."

Neither woman said anything after that for a long moment. Moira's mind was racing. *Why* would Cameron kill Zander? What motive could he have? Her gaze fell on Jenny's face, and she realized that his motive was standing right in front of her.

Cameron was in love with Jenny, by his own admission. He had spent the last six months trying to get her to notice him, trying to get her to like him for who he was, not just his money. After Jenny and Zander broke up for the first time, he must have been relieved and thought he had a chance with her. But if he somehow found out that they had begun seeing each other again...

"Jenny, where is Cameron now?"

"He's over at the reception hall. I—I was scared to be there alone with him, or I would have waited to tell you. I don't want to wreck your wedding."

"Don't worry about that. If you're right, then you just solved Zander's murder and cleared my name. I could hug you—but I won't, because Freya will murder *me* if I smudge this makeup."

Moira slipped back into the dressing room, then hesitated. She had been about to grab her phone and call David... but was that really the best thing to do? He would be just as busy preparing for the wedding as she was supposed to be. If she could somehow get Cameron safely in police custody without disturbing the ceremony, that would be ideal.

She glanced at the clock. In forty-five minutes, she was supposed to get married. The reception hall—

really just the event center at City Hall—was only a five-minute drive away. She could go there and... and what? And get Cameron to confess. If she could somehow convince Detective Jefferson to go along with her, he could arrest the young man on the spot, all in time for her to get back to the church before the ceremony began.

"I'll be right back," she told a startled Martha as she pushed past her to grab her purse. "Don't let them start without me."

CHAPTER SIXTEEN

"Wait!" Jenny called as Moira rushed down the church's hallway. "I want to come with you."

The deli owner hesitated for a moment before biting her lip and agreeing. "I have a plan; I'll explain it to you on the way. But I've got to make a call first. Can you drive?"

They ran through the parking lot, Moira slowing down just enough to hoist up her skirts as she hurried across the asphalt. She leapt into the passenger seat and tossed Jenny her keys. "Head to the reception hall," she said before pulling out her cell phone and scrolling down to Detective Jefferson's number.

They pulled into the City Hall parking lot a few minutes later, both women frightened but determined. An unmarked black car pulled in after them a moment later. It cruised by in front of them close enough for her to recognize Detective Jefferson, and she felt a rush of relief. He hadn't liked her plan, but at least he had believed her enough to meet them there.

"Are you sure you want to do this?" she asked Jenny.

"I'm sure," the young woman said. "I think you're right—if he's going to confess to anyone, it'll be to me."

"Let's go, then. David will never forgive me if I'm late to our wedding."

They edged their way into the eerily empty City Hall building and began making their way towards the stairway that led down to the event center. It had been over a year since Moira had been there. In fact, the last time she had been there had been a retirement party for a detective... a detective that had been killed later that night.

Maybe it wasn't such a good idea to host the reception here, she thought with a shiver. *The last time I went to an event held here, it didn't exactly end well.*

"Are you ready?" she asked Jenny at the top of the stairs. They could hear the sounds of conversation from the basement. Moira had forgotten that Allison would be there too.

"Ready," the other woman said. "Are you sure that detective will be nearby?"

"He'll be close," Moira promised. "And the second

he hears Cameron confess, he'll step in and arrest him."

"Okay." She took a deep breath. "Here we go."

The two of them walked down the stairs to find a beautifully decorated reception hall waiting for them. Allison and Cameron were on the far side of the room, pulling a table cloth over the long table that the cake would be presented on. Strings of beautiful white lights hung all around, giving the room an almost magical look.

"Ahem," Jenny said. Cameron and Allison looked around, both of their faces taking on the same shocked expression when they saw Moira standing there in her wedding dress.

"What's going on, Ms. D? Did something happen to the wedding?" Allison asked.

"No, it's still on," the deli owner assured her grimly. "But we need to talk to Cameron... alone, if that's all right."

The other woman looked between them, confused, but agreed to give them some privacy. "I need to get the place cards from the truck anyway," she said, excusing herself. Moira waited until she had disappeared up the stairs before turning back to Cameron.

The young man was looking at Jenny with a resigned look on his face. "Look, I think I know what this is about... I just don't want it to change things between us, Jenny."

"What do you mean, you don't want it to 'change things'?" the brunette asked in a high-pitched voice. "How can you be so calm about this? I know what you did! Ms. D knows what you did. You're a terrible person, Cam."

Moira put a hand on Jenny's arm, trying to calm her down. *We just need a confession,* she thought. *Focus on getting that, Jenny... come on...*

"What—what did I do wrong?" Cameron asked, stumbling back from her outburst in confusion. "Maybe I should have told you right off the bat, but like I told Ms. D, I wanted you to like me for me, not for my money."

"What are you talking about?" Jenny said, staring at him with a blank look on her face. "Are you saying... did you get *paid* to kill him?"

"What?" the young man gaped at her. "I didn't kill anyone!"

He really sounds surprised, the deli owner thought. *Could we be wrong? Jenny's theory had made so much sense, though.*

"Yes, you did," Jenny snapped. "Ms. D and I figured it all out. You saw Cameron the night before he died, and then those police officers asked me all of those questions, and they took your fingerprints—"

"Jenny, I didn't kill him. How can you even think that? I thought this was about my money."

"What money?"

He looked at Moira, who nodded encouragement. Cameron blew out a slow breath, then said, "Jenny... I'm rich. Like, really rich. I didn't want to tell you... well, because I like you. A lot. Most of the women I've dated in the past haven't really been into *me,* I don't think most of them would have even looked at me if I had been some poor guy. With you, I wanted to give something real a chance to develop." He gave dry chuckle. "I guess it turns out that I'm pretty terrible at flirting when I don't have my money to back me up. I don't think you ever looked at me as more than a coworker."

175

"Cameron... is this true?"

"It's true that he has money," Moira said. "He's the one that paid my bail. I know what he's saying about his feelings for you is also true. He's been working at the deli for the last six months just to be near you."

"But... but what about Zander?" the young woman asked. "If you... if you really like me that much, then that would give you even more reason to want to kill him. You knew we were getting back together. I told you as much just a couple of days before he died."

"I didn't kill Zander," Cameron said firmly. "Jenny, I would never hurt someone you care about."

Jenny and Moira exchanged a glance. He *seemed* sincere enough. The deli owner thought back all the months she had known him, and couldn't remember ever seeing him get violent or angry. She thought that he did honestly care for the young woman standing next to her, that wasn't something he could fake.

"I... I think he's telling the truth, Ms. D," Jenny said.

"I think so, too." She winced at the thought of the conversation she would probably be having with Detective Jefferson shortly. He was bound to be annoyed by the false alarm.

"You should get back to your wedding," Jenny said. She glanced over at Cameron. "I'm going to stay here. We've got a lot to talk about."

Moira nodded. "Cameron... I'm sorry." She turned to face her employee, embarrassed.

"Don't worry about it, Ms. D. I guess it's good the

cat's out of the bag now. I shouldn't keep secrets from someone I care about."

She nodded, shot one more glance towards Jenny, who gave her a reassuring smile, then turned and headed towards the stairs. *At least David isn't here,* she thought. She would have been even more embarrassed than she already was if her fiancé had witnessed her wrongly accusing one of her employees of murder. Detective Jefferson witnessing it was bad enough.

He joined her at the top of the stairs, looking amused. "That was a real brutal killer you uncovered."

"Oh, hush," she told him. "I'm getting married today —you have to be nice to me. Tomorrow you can give me the lecture about wasting valuable police resources if you want."

"Nah," he said. "I did this on my own time. I was *supposed* to be getting ready to attend a certain deli owner's wedding, actually. I guess I don't have time to change now... I'll just have to wear jeans."

"Shoot," Moira said, pulling out her phone. "I've only got ten minutes until I'm supposed to be walking down the aisle!"

She hurried to her car, hoisted her skirts, and got in the driver's seat. Solving Zander's murder would just have to wait one more day—right now, she had vows to make.

CHAPTER SEVENTEEN

Moira pulled into the church parking lot with only minutes to spare. She closed her eyes and took a deep breath, gripping the steering wheel tightly. This was it. In just a few minutes, she would be walking down the aisle towards David, and within an hour she would leave the church as a married woman.

"Breathe," she told herself. She pulled down the visor and examined her face and hair in the little mirror. Freya hadn't quite gotten a chance to finish her eyeshadow, but it wasn't noticeable. Her hair was still in place, and her makeup remained unsmudged. She smiled at herself in the mirror, then flipped the visor back up. It was time to find Martha and her other bridesmaids... all of whom were probably a wee bit upset with her for running off as she had.

She got out of the car, hit the button on her keys to lock it, and started towards the church. Halfway across the parking lot, she paused. Barely visible around the corner of the church was the nose of a black van. A van just like the one that she had seen the morning of Zander's murder.

She looked from the van to the church doors, then back again. *Just go inside,* she told herself. *I can tell Jefferson about the van after the wedding.* But what if the van was gone by then? It wouldn't take her more than a few seconds to dash around the corner and take a photo of the van's license plate. Then Detective Jefferson could track down its owner at his leisure. *Getting that plate number could clear my name.* That thought made her mind up. She pulled out her phone and hurried around the corner.

Heart pounding, she walked slowly around the van,

keeping alert in case its owner came back. When she had circled around it to the license plate, she pulled open the camera app on her phone and quickly snapped a picture. *Dang it, it was blurry.* Her hand was shaking with pre-wedding jitters, making it difficult to get a good picture. With a sigh, she tried again. The second picture was clear enough that she could at least make out the numbers. *The police probably have something they can use to sharpen the image if they have to*, she thought.

She straightened up and slid her phone back into her purse. *That was easy. Now, it's time to get married.* She took one step back towards the front of the church when the van's big door rolled open. With a yelp, the deli owner jumped back.

"Oh, it's you," she said, feeling a mixture of annoyance and disappointment. Brendan Anaheim, the reporter, was frowning at her from the van. *I really thought I had found the killer's vehicle*, she thought with a sigh. *But it's just a stupid news van.*

"What are you doing back here?" Brendan asked, eyeing her suspiciously.

"I was just taking a walk. It's my wedding," she pointed out. "What are *you* doing here?"

"It's your wedding." He gave her a nasty grin. "There's bound to be a good story here. You're our viewers' favorite suspect for Zander Marsh's murder, and you're getting married today while out on bail that an extremely wealthy employee posted. People would *kill* to watch this."

"Watch it?" she asked. "What do you mean? You're not recording my wedding."

She saw his eyes flick upwards reflexively, and followed his gaze. Above the van was a small window that, if her mental map of the church was right, would be overlooking the ceremony.

"Boss, I found a ladder in the shed." Moira spun around to find herself face to face with a very surprised cameraman carrying an aluminum extendible ladder.

"Thanks, Rodney, but I don't think we'll need it any more. I've got a better idea." Brendan's nasty grin widened. "Grab her."

"Wha—" Moira yelped as Rodney dropped the ladder and grabbed her by the arms.

"Into the van, boss?"

"Yep. I think I'm more in the mood for a kidnapping than a wedding. Aren't you?"

"Help!" The deli owner took a deep breath to yell again, but the cameraman slapped a hand over her mouth. Brendan came forward to help wrestle her into the van, easily avoiding her kicks and flailing arms.

Once inside the black van, Rodney slammed the door shut, then grabbed a roll of tape from a shelf. Brendan held her firmly while Rodney bound her wrists behind her back.

"You drive," he told the cameraman once they were done. "Head towards the lake."

The van started and moved forward with a lurch. Moira was staring around at the interior with wide eyes. The van was chock-full of equipment: recording devices, television screens, and an odd-looking handheld miniature satellite.

"Our sound amplifier," Brendan said, looking at it fondly. "Government-grade, of course."

"I don't understand," Moira said, tugging at the tape behind her back. "Why are you doing this? I'm not going to let you get away with it. The second you let me go, I'm going to the police. There will be a big story, all right, but about you two, not me. I'm missing my wedding because of you!"

Brendan shook his head slowly. "Moira, Moira, Moira. We aren't letting you go. Imagine this head-line—*Murderer Succumbs to Guilt on Wedding Day, Commits Suicide.* We'll be the first reporters on the scene when they find your body in the lake. This story will be *mine.* Beyond News will finally get national recognition. We won't be a small local channel for much longer. This story is going to go *viral.*"

"You're crazy," the deli owner said. "You can't just kill someone for a news story—"

She broke off, realizing something that suddenly seemed glaringly obvious to her.

"You already did, didn't you? You killed Zander."

It all made sense. This *was* the same van that she had seen at Zander's that morning. Brendan must have been watching, waiting for her to show up so he could give her description to the police. If he had committed the crime, it would explain how he knew some of the information that he had, though not all of it.

"I'm surprised you put it together so fast," he said.

"Why him? I don't understand."

Brendan shrugged. "It wasn't anything personal. I've had this idea for a while, in fact—to create the story that I wanted to report on, instead of just waiting for it to happen. Zander Marsh just happened to be a convenient target. I was at his office doing an interview about his microbrewery, and I happened to see on his schedule that he had a meeting with you set up. Now, your name is a pretty familiar one in my circles. You've been implicated in crimes before. Something just seemed to click. It made perfect sense—kill him, pin it on you, and report on all of the ensuing chaos. It went perfectly. I showed up an hour before you were supposed to get there and surprised him at his desk. He pulled a gun on me, but that turned out to be perfect. I wrestled it away from him, shot him twice, wiped it clean, and dropped it. You actually picking it up went beyond anything I expected. I loved you for that."

"How do you know I picked it up?" she asked him. "Who's your source? If you're going to kill me anyway, you might as well tell me." She winced as the van went over a bump. She was still struggling with the tape on her wrists, but didn't seem to be making much progress.

"I don't need a source at the police station," he said proudly. "I got all of the information myself, using that beauty over there." He pointed to the sound amplifier. "It's summer, and your detectives like to sit in the break room with the window open while they're discussing their cases. I learned a *lot* by hiding in the bushes with the amplifier."

"You're crazy," the deli owner said. "Is a good news story really worth killing two people over?"

"Money, fame, my own show on a big network... you bet it is."

"Uh, boss? We've got a problem," said Rodney from the front.

"What is it?" Brendan snapped.

"Someone's tailing us."

Moira felt a spark of hope. Had someone noticed them kidnap her?

"Well, lose them," the reporter said.

"How? We're in a huge van. They're in a car. I can't exactly outrun them."

"I don't know! Go off road if you have to."

Brendan gripped a rail installed in the back of the van for stability, then put his other hand on Moira's shoulder. "This may get bumpy."

Bumpy was an understatement. Rodney yanked the wheel to the left, and the van jumped up on the curb, then smashed through something wooden. Moira winced as a laptop flew off of one of the shelves and clipped her in the calf.

"Oh, crud!"

The van came to a sudden, brutal stop, sending both Moira and Brendan flying forward. Dazed, the deli owner struggled to her feet, shaking chunks of broken glass off of herself. The reporter was groaning on the floor, clutching a bloody arm. Rodney, still in the driver's seat, was beating back an airbag.

The deli owner staggered to the van's sliding door and wrestled it open. She got out of the vehicle as quickly as she dared, trying to figure out if she was actually okay, or if she was in shock from some horrible injury that she hadn't noticed yet. *I have all my limbs,* she thought. *I don't think I'm bleeding. What on earth just happened?*

She looked around. They were in a field dotted with bushes and trees. A cow lowed at her from only a few yards away. The van's nose was completely crushed in—it had smashed into a stump hidden in a clump of tall grass. She was beginning to hear more sounds of movement from inside the vehicle now; Brendan was shouting at Rodney.

"You idiot! You had one job, and you screwed it up. I should have hired that foreign guy. You crashed my van! That woman is getting away... *and* I think my arm is broken."

"Dude, you gotta help me," Rodney said. "My legs are stuck. I can't get out."

"Screw you. I've gotta go catch that chick before she runs to the police."

Moira turned back the way that they had come from, desperately looking for somewhere to run to. She saw the splintered fence that the van had broken through and started towards it, pulling her skirts up so she could run without tripping over them.

She heard footsteps in the grass behind her and ran faster, hoping that Brendan's broken arm would slow him down enough for her to get to the road before he did. Not daring to look back, she ran as fast as she could... stumbling to a stop only when she saw a familiar unmarked police vehicle roll through the hole in the fence. Red and blue lights flashed from a hidden strip on the car's roof. Moira heard a muffled curse from behind her, and turned to see Brendan turning tail and running back towards the wrecked van.

"Moira!" a familiar voice called out to her. "Are you okay?"

She hurried forward to meet Detective Jefferson, who had gotten out of his car and was running the last few feet towards her.

"I'm fine," she panted. "But they're going to get away! You have to stop them. It's that reporter, Brendan, and his cameraman. They killed Zander."

"They won't be going anywhere," Jefferson assured her with a grim smile. "I called for backup, they should be here any minute."

Moira could hear sirens in the distance, drawing ever nearer. "Thank goodness," she breathed. "How did you find me?"

"I was only a few seconds behind you, remember? I followed you back from City Hall, but got cut off by a stoplight. I pulled in to the parking lot in time to see you walk around the corner of the church building. I didn't think much of it—I thought you were heading towards a side entrance—until I saw that van pull out and speed off a moment later. I wasn't sure you were in it, of course, but I tailed it anyway. When I saw the van go off road and into this cow field, I knew something was really wrong. Are you sure you're all right?"

The deli owner nodded, then gasped. "David! The wedding! What time is it?"

She peered at the detective's watch and felt a sinking feeling in the pit of her stomach. She was late, her hair was a mess, and she had broken glass in her dress.

"What am I going to do?" She felt tears prickle her eyes. All of this, and she was going to miss her own wedding.

"Get in my car and call your maid of honor. I'm sure she can come up with something. I'll escort you back just as soon as I make sure those two get arrested."

It was a plan, at least. Moira took his phone, punched in Martha's number, and tried to think of what on earth she would tell her friend.

CHAPTER EIGHTEEN

The first notes of the bridal march began, signaling that it was time for Moira to make her appearance. She took a deep breath, clutched her flowers, and stepped through the doors into the cathedral. Her eyes immediately found David, who was gazing at her with a rapt expression on his face. He looked relieved, and she could imagine why. The wedding had been delayed for another half hour while Freya did her best to fix the damage that had been done to Moira's hair and makeup during the crazy van ride. She still wasn't sure quite what explanation Martha had given to the people assembled for the wedding, but it seemed to have worked because no one had left.

As she walked she looked slowly around the room at all of the people that had gathered there to watch her and David exchange vows. Candice, Denise, Martha, and Karissa were all standing near David, watching her with smiles on their faces. Detective Jefferson, who had come in nearly as late as she, was seated near the back, and winked at her as she walked by. She knew he was thinking of the story that she would be telling David as soon as the wedding was over. Her groom might have a heart attack when he found out that his bride had been kidnapped less than an hour before walking down the aisle.

Her eyes found David's mother on the other side of the church. To her surprise, the woman gave her an encouraging smile, which Moira returned. *She still thinks I'm a troublemaker*, the deli owner knew. *And once she hears about this, her opinion definitely won't be improving.* But at least the older woman seemed to appreciate the fact that Moira made David happy, and hopefully that would be enough to keep the relationship with her mother in law a good one.

Her gaze was drawn back to David. He looked wonderful in his new suit, with a fresh haircut and shave. His eyes never once wavered from her, and a blush rose in her cheeks at the intensity of his expression. He was looking at her like she was the most important person in the world.

At last she took the final steps and handed her bouquet to Candice. She met David's gaze with an eager smile of her own. Now that she was up here, her nerves were gone. She was ready for the vows.

"David, will you take Moira Darling to be your wife? Do you promise to love, honor, and trust her in sickness and in health, for richer or for poorer, for better or for worse, and to be true and loyal to her so long as you both shall live?"

"I do," her fiancé said, holding her gaze.

The minister turned to her. "Moira, will you take

PATTI BENNING

David Morris to be your husband? Do you promise to love, honor, and trust him in sickness and in health, for richer or for poorer, for better or for worse, and to be true and loyal to him so long as you both shall live?"

"I do," she said, smiling up at the man that she loved.

The wedding party moved to the reception hall after the vows and rings had finished being exchanged. Moira, giddy at the thought that she was now a married woman, held tightly to David's hand as they mingled with their friends. She had decided that she would wait to tell him about the kidnapping until later tonight, not wanting to wreck the wonderful day by making him worry about her.

The reception hall was beautiful. Allison, Cameron, and Jenny had obviously been hard at work while the others were at the wedding. There wasn't a surface that wasn't decorated, or a table setting that wasn't perfect. The three-tiered cake, which had been delivered moments before the guests arrived, was absolutely gorgeous. Covered in white chocolate buttercream frosting, and decorated with artful flowers, it looked like something that Moira would see in a magazine. It would almost be a shame to cut into it... almost. The promise of the layers of fresh strawberry and rich chocolate cake under the frosting was enough to make her mouth water.

The rest of the food looked amazing, too. The deli's three volunteers had really gone all out. Platters of cold cuts and cheese were laid out on the long table, along with a variety of fresh sliced bread, bowls of fruit, heated pots of soup, and even a champagne tower.

At the other end of the room was a DJ and a live band, still setting up. Part of the hall had been sectioned off for dancing, and Moira couldn't wait to get out on the dance floor with her new husband.

"Oh, Mom, that was a beautiful ceremony," Candice

said, approaching them with Eli at her side. "Everything was just perfect. I'm so happy for both of you."

"Thanks, sweetie. You were wonderful. You look so
beautiful in your dress." She embraced her daughter
while Eli congratulated David. "I can't wait to see
what you two do for your wedding."

Candice grinned. "Me either. It's going to be fun to
plan. Will you help?"

"Of course."

They were interrupted by Martha, who was weaving
her way through the crows towards them. She gave
Moira a wide-eyed look.

"Were you being serious on the phone?" she asked.
"I spent the whole ceremony trying to figure out if

you were, or if you had been playing some weird joke on me."

"Trust me, I was a hundred percent serious," Moira told her. She glanced at the others. "I'll tell you all about it, but later, okay? I just want to enjoy being married right now."

During her panicked call from Detective Jefferson's car, she had told Martha everything. Her friend was the only one that knew why she had really been late, and she knew the other woman was probably dying to hear a more detailed version of the story.

"What are you two talking about?" David asked, looking between them. "What *did* happen back there? I was worried you had gotten cold feet."

"Your wife is crazy," Martha said, shaking her head in amazement. "That's all I'll say."

Moira grinned and kissed David on the cheek. "I'll tell you later, all right? I promise... everything is good now. No cold feet. Ever."

He opened his mouth to object, but she cut him off with another kiss. There would be enough time to talk about kidnappings and murderers later. For now, she wanted to kiss her husband, get a piece of cake, and enjoy the happiest night of her life.

Book 33: Murder, My Darling

Killer Cookie Series

Book 1: Killer Caramel Cookies

Book 2: Killer Halloween Cookies

Book 3: Killer Maple Cookies

Book 4: Crunchy Christmas Murder

Book 5: Killer Valentine Cookies

Asheville Meadows Series

Book 1: Small Town Murder

Book 2: Murder on Aisle Three

Book 3: The Heart of Murder

Book 4: Dating is Murder

Book 5: Dying to Cook

Book 6: Food, Family and Murder

Book 7: Fish, Chips and Murder

Cozy Mystery Tails of Alaska

Book 1: Mushing is Murder

AUTHOR'S NOTE

I'd love to hear your thoughts on my books, the storylines, and anything else that you'd like to comment on—reader feedback is very important to me. My contact information, along with some other helpful links, is listed on the next page. If you'd like to be on my list of "folks to contact" with updates, release and sales notifications, etc.... just shoot me an email and let me know. Thanks for reading!

Also...

... if you're looking for more great reads, Summer Prescott Books publishes several popular series by outstanding Cozy Mystery authors.

CONTACT SUMMER PRESCOTT BOOKS PUBLISHING

Twitter: @summerprescott1

Bookbub:
https://www.bookbub.com/authors/summer-prescott

Blog and Book Catalog:
http://summerprescottbooks.com

Email: summer.prescott.cozies@gmail.com

YouTube:
https://www.youtube.com/channel/UCngKNUkDd
WuQ5k7-Vkfrp6A

And...be sure to check out the Summer Prescott Cozy Mysteries fan page and Summer Prescott Books Publishing Page on Facebook – let's be friends!

To download a free book, and sign up for our fun and exciting newsletter, which will give you opportunities to win prizes and swag, enter contests, and be the first to know about New Releases, click here: http://summerprescottbooks.com

Made in the USA
Las Vegas, NV
13 September 2024

95220182R00125